A NEW DEPUTY

"The pay's standard, five hundred a year plus two dollars per arrest. You'll never get rich and you may get killed. Still want the job?"

"Yes, sir."

"On your feet and raise your right hand. Do you, Miss Frances Hatch, solemnly swear to abide by the laws of Lipscomb County and the State of Texas and defend and protect the citizens of Lipscomb County and their property at the risk of your life?"

"I do."

"Then I hereby appoint you my deputy sheriff."

He moved to pin the badge on. He slowed his hands and stopped them an inch from her bulging breast pocket . . .

The FANCY HATCH series from Pinnacle Books

#1 FANCY HATCH
#2 THE CASE DEUCE
#3 SOLOMON KING'S MINE
#4 THE ODDS AGAINST SUNDOWN

#4

ZACHARY HAWKES

THE ODDS AGAINST SUNDOWN

PINNACLE BOOKS NEW YORK

> **ATTENTION: SCHOOLS AND CORPORATIONS**
>
> PINNACLE Books are available at quantity discounts with bulk purchases for educational, business or special promotional use. For further details, please write to: SPECIAL SALES MANAGER, Pinnacle Books, Inc., 1430 Broadway, New York, NY 10018.

This novel is a work of fiction. Names, characters, places, and incidents are either the product of the author's imagination or are used fictitiously. Any resemblance to actual events or places or persons, living or dead, is entirely coincidental.

FANCY HATCH #4: THE ODDS AGAINST SUNDOWN

Copyright © 1985 by Alan Riefe

All rights reserved, including the right to reproduce this book or portions thereof in any form.

An original Pinnacle Books edition, published for the first time anywhere.

First printing/March 1985

ISBN: 0-523-42137-0
Can. ISBN: 0-523-43131-7

Printed in the United States of America

PINNACLE BOOKS, INC.
1430 Broadway
New York, New York 10018

9   8   7   6   5   4   3   2   1

THE ODDS AGAINST SUNDOWN

One

Her horse, Lady, a feisty and rugged little Spanish Barb, was anything but feisty at the moment. She had picked up a pebble about half a mile out of town and, try as Fancy might, she could not reach it with the point of her knife to pry it from under the shoe. She led Lady limping into Lipscomb, looking for the blacksmith. Crossing the Oklahoma–Texas border and the trickle that was all that remained of Kiowa Creek some thirty-five miles back, she had spared her horse, riding at an unhurried but steady gait. It was early July and sweltering, much too hot for beast or man. The brutal tyrant sun ruling the sky poured its heat down like molten metal. The back of Fancy's silk shirt was dark with sweat; it coursed down the nape of her neck and down her face, salting her eyes, setting them stinging. She felt as if shirt, denims and boots were glued to her, that any attempt on her part to remove her shirt in particular would be as painful as stripping off court plaster. Not a breath of air stirred. Dust raised by the horse hung above the narrow, deeply rutted road. This was wheat country, great seas of it spreading as far as she could see, standing completely motionless, as if every stalk were frozen.

She shook her canteen; it was empty. She knew it was before she shook it, but so thirsty was she, her throat feeling as if it were layered with hot dust, wishful thinking prompted her to double check for water.

The broiling sun held Lipscomb in thrall. The road widened to become its main, its only, street, then narrowed again as the buildings gave out left and right of it. Such was Lipscomb, small, tiny, fewer than two hundred residents, a place where the wheat farmers and their help could gather on Saturday nights, a stage stop boasting the customary assortment of necessary business establishments, a solitary saloon, formidable solid brick bank, a stable adjacent to the blacksmith's shop. The newest, most attractive building, two stories, white-painted clapboarding which, reflected Fancy, would not remain white for long in this part of the country, was the Lipscomb House Hotel. Her second stop after the smith's.

The street was competely deserted, not even a stray dog or cat in sight. The tinkling of a piano in the Bird Cage Saloon became faintly audible as she entered town. Upstairs over the general store out of an open window came a woman's shrill berating voice. The pianist and the chastiser were the only proof that Lipscomb was not a ghost town. It was nearing one o'clock in the afternoon, the sun only beginning to desert its zenith. Lipscombians clearly had no desire to challenge its fierceness, not until the shadows arrived and the bully had shed its glare and most of its heat and begun settling behind the Sangre de Cristo mountains to the west. Only then would the populace emerge from within.

The town sat on the southern bank of Wolf Creek, like Kiowa Creek to the north reduced to a trickle and threatening to dry up completely by the time August arrived.

The steady *clink, clink, clink* of metal on metal drew her attention to the shed attached to the livery stable. The smith was young, barely twenty, she guessed, displaying behind his apron the usual physical equipment with which all in the trade are endowed, including her Uncle Justin back in Noel, Missouri. It was he who had skillfully fashioned for her the steel-reinforced gloves she wore that looked like ordinary calfskin riding gloves. She called them "mother's little helpers"; they were her "equalizer." She had learned to ride and rope and shoot, pistol, rifle, shotgun as well as any man, but when called upon to defend her honor, cash or few worldly goods with her fists she would have been at a serious disadvantage wearing ordinary gloves.

She also wore a Peacemaker on her shapely hip and in a scabbard against Lady's right shoulder reposed a 10-gauge shotgun. She had come from Topeka, Kansas to Lipscomb, a distance of better than three hundred and fifty miles for a definite purpose. Though, to be honest, the long, difficult, exhausting trek was itself, a cross-your-fingers-and-hope-you-strike-gold challenge. She had heard a rumor, and that was all it really was, that the man she was looking for had drifted down to Texas and located in or near Lipscomb. His name was Moss Kilbane. He was in his thirties and stood well over six feet. He affected a railroad hat and an expensive, custom-made broadcloth suit. He also wore handlebar mustaches; he had evil eyes, a clear and devious mind and the conscience of a starving rattler.

He had murdered her fiance Richard Ainsley in cold blood. He had shot her in the same encounter. The single bullet had lodged a scant inch under her heart. She had been confined to bed for eighteen days. She had very nearly died; the fact that she did not astonished the doctor who removed the slug. It astonished her Aunt Tabitha and Uncle Justin as well; not Fancy. She came out of her delirium with a purpose, an obligation, a mandatory mission for the years to come; find the well-dressed man with the handlebar mustaches who, fleeing the local bank with his friends, had passed the buggy in which she and Richard were riding to the church on their wedding day. Kilbane had pulled up sharply, fired three shots point blank into the back of Richard (who had thrown himself protectingly over her). When Richard fell dead, the killer fired a fourth shot directly at her at a range of less than twenty feet. So close had he been she could not understand what had prevented the bullet from passing through her.

He had smirked, a death's-head leer, then laughed and galloped off. And her wedding day had become the blackest of her life. Even before she fully recovered she vowed to find Kilbane and revenge herself. She had succeeded in catching up with him three different times, but one way or another he had managed to elude her. And so her quest went on and would until the book could be closed.

The ride down had consumed almost ten days. Would he still be here or was he long gone? Had he even arrived here? Was he anyplace within two hundred miles? Questions, doubts, and pessimism continually assailed her, but even a rumor, as flimsy as rumors could be, was something to go on. It suggested, at least, the *possibility* of finding him.

He led two lives, galloping about the territories turning over banks, express offices and anything else for a quick and easy profit. He also dealt faro. His second life would, she had long ago decided, eventually prove his downfall. Her reason for thinking so was that dealing faro obliged him to stay in one place, usually for a fairly extended length of time.

The smith greeted her: sweat poured off him. He was

handsome: blond, curly hair, twinkling, mischievous dark blue eyes, skin deeply tanned. He noticed Lady, and his smile fell into a look of sympathy. He set down his hammer and tongs and came out and took her reins. He examined the shoe.

"A stone," said Fancy.

"Can happen. Let's get her inside." He ruffled Lady's mane. "Uncomfortable, isn't it, lil' gal?"

Positioning her to his satisfaction, he bent over and lifted her hoof between his legs.

"Minneola bar. Good shoe. I'll jus' loosen it a mite and we'll get that pesky pebble outta there pronto. Hand me that iron, ma'am. . . ."

"Fancy, Fancy Hatch."

"Luther Coombs. Pleased and pleasured to know you. You and her look like you've come all the way from Canady. I bet you're thirsty. There's well water in that bucket on the wall. "See the dipper handle? Help yourself, and Lady too."

"Thank you."

She drank and poured a quantity into her hat. Lady downed it greedily. So cold was it, Fancy paused at least ten seconds between gulps. Luther, meanwhile, loosened the shoe and out fell the pebble. He loosened the nail nearest where it had lodged a little more and examined the hoof for injury.

"No harm done."

The shoe was hammered back into place. Lady put her down hoof tentatively, her eyes widening, but when she felt no discomfort she lifted it and set it down a couple of times.

"We both thank you," said Fancy, "thank the Lord we were fairly close to town when it happened. How much do I owe you?"

"For thirty seconds work? Not a red cent."

"Please, let me pay. . . ."

He held up his hands defensively. "Not on your tintype."

"Luther . . ."

It was not Fancy who spoke, although she was about to insist that he permit her to pay him something. She turned. A pretty blonde with cornflower blue eyes, shining cheeks and perfect teeth stood smiling in the doorway. She wore a lovely hand-embroidered hoopless, straight-skirted cotton dress with a tiny red-and black-lozenge pattern running horizontally to form a belt at the waist. Fancy could not avoid a fleeting feeling of envy. It had been months since she herself had worn the dress made for her by Aunt Tabitha; it was neatly folded, reposing in her saddlebag, along with a pair of plain white slippers. She was continually promising herself that she would put them on if only to see herself briefly in the nearest mirror at least once every week, wherever she was, whatever she was doing, preferably in the privacy of her hotel room in the next town her pursuit of Kilbane brought her to, but for one reason or another she never seemed to get around to it.

"Excuse me, Miss, for interrupting . . ."

"Maude," said Luther, "this here is Fancy Hatch just come to town from a thousand mile away, as you can plainly see, and this is her horse Lady, who Dr. Coombs has just finished fixing good as new." He fastened his eyes on Fancy and pushed his head forward like a chicken. "For nothing, no charge, favor to a Lady in distress. You get that, ladies? Lady's her horse, Maude. Oh, Fancy, this is Miss Maude Catlett. Soon to become Mrs., worse luck for all us eligible bachelors in town."

Fancy noticed that Maude was wearing a tiny diamond. Luther's reference reminded her to display her ring more prominently and with pride. She placed her hand across her breast.

"Pleased to meet you, Fancy," she said. They shook hands. "Luther, did you get around to fixing my bridle yet?"

"As best I could. You might think 'bout buying a new one, Maude. That bridle musta come west with Zebulon Pike. I got to have repaired it at least twenty times. It's just gonna break on you again, you know."

"I can't afford a new one, Luther Coombs, if it's all the same to you. I'm saving every penny I get. A new bridle costs more than two dollars."

"Hogwash, I can get you one brand new, that is hardly used, for half that." He lowered his voice. "Old man Hampton next door's just tryin' to bleed you, chargin' two dollars for a dumb bridle, the old skinflint."

"You bet he's an old skinflint," agreed Maude, not lowering her voice, causing Luther to wince.

"Hush up, he's got ears like a mule deer."

He got her bridle and showed her where he had repaired it.

"How much?" she asked.

"Twenty-five cents should do it."

"How about twenty?"

"Aw for gosh sakes, Maude, I done you a favor! Leather stitching's not even my line. The only reason I do it is 'cause I know you don't like doin' business with . . ." He tilted his head sharply toward the stable next door.

"I sure don't." She got out a quarter and handed it to him.

"Wait there, I'll get your change . . ."

"What change?"

"Your nickel."

"You said twenty-five cents; that's what I gave you, you ninny!"

"I know what I said. I know too I'll never hear the end o' it from Miss Pinchpenny if . . ."

"Keep the foolish nickel; don't start jawing with me!"

"Okay, all right! If you two'll excuse me, I got a wheel to mount. For . . ." Again he tilted his head sharply. "If he doesn't get it back this afternoon he'll raise holy hannah. Pleasure makin' your 'quaintance, Fancy. Come see us again. Get a pebble in your boot, I'll take it out."

"Fresh!" snapped Maude.

"Just funnin', Maude, for gosh sakes."

Maude, with her bridle, and Fancy, with Lady trailing her, set off down the street. They talked, hitting it off famously within minutes, an almost instant friendship; two polar personalities complementing one another perfectly. Chemistry was all when it came to people. Maude was all questions as to where she had come from, and why to Lipscomb "of all places." Without a moment's hesitation, trusting her on sight, Fancy divulged her reason. She described Kilbane in detail. As they slowly walked along, Maude listened, but her pretty face darkened in a frown and she shook her head.

"Nobody around here looks like that. Nobody I know, and I know everybody. Lived here all my life."

"He could be lying low someplace out of town."

"Is there any way he'd know you've come down here looking for him?"

"I don't think so."

"*Why* are you looking for him, Fancy?"

"He murdered my fiance and shot and nearly killed me," she announced flatly.

Maude gasped. "The rotten stinker! What will you do when you catch up with him?"

"Try my best to keep from emptying both guns into him on the spot. Collar him and turn him over to the law. Although," she added dryly, "he does have the most discouraging knack for squirming out of the law's hold whenever it gets a hand on him. I'll decide what to do with him when I catch up with him."

"If . . . ?"

"*When.*" She stopped, taking Maude by the arm. "Please do me a favor, don't say anything about him to anybody. Promise?"

"I could ask around. Could be somebody saw him."

"I'd rather you didn't. If he is here it would only alert him. He'd love to catch up with me. He'd like me dead as badly as I'd like him." She chuckled grimly. "I guess we're two of a kind."

"Hardly, from what you've told me."

An ancient gray hound loped tiredly across the street in front of them, dragging its legs as if each step was to be its last. He'd made it to the shade in front of Beazley's General Store.

"Where you staying?"

"The hotel, I guess."

"You aren't. It looks nice from the outside, but it's grubby in. They don't clean the rooms but once a week and the lobby reeks of cigar smoke."

"Doesn't every?"

"You get sick to your stomach walking from the door to the desk. Huygen Willis, the manager, never opens the front windows to let the breeze in."

"What breeze is that?" asked Fancy smiling.

"Oh, the wind'll come up when the sun goes down. Huygen Willis is the town slob. Small wonder the hotel's a holy mess." She brightened, suddenly possessed of an idea. "You're coming home with me! You can have the spare room. Mother and Daddy won't mind a whit; they'll be happy to have company."

"That's very generous of you, Maude, but I couldn't impose . . ."

"You wouldn't be imposing. Please come!"

"We've just met. We hardly know each other . . ."

"What's that got to do with anything? We're already best friends." She snapped her fingers and grinned. "Just like that. You're a stranger in town, you need a friend. So do I, my best friend Annie Shockley moved to Austin, the stinker. Just 'cause her husband got a job there." She tittered. I'm only fooling. Annie was a good soul, I miss her. You've got to take her place, Miss Fancy Hatch . . ." She paused and eyed her. "Is Fancy your real name?"

"Frances. I picked up Fancy when I was little. It stuck. Maude, you're very kind; it's very thoughtful of you, but I can't stay with you. I came to Lipscomb for one reason only, to find Kilbane. If I do, things could get hot and heavy in a hurry. If he *is* here and I can find him, I'll have things my way, it'll be my game. If he's here and he gets wind that I am, he'll come after me. Then it becomes *his* game. Either way, it's a dangerous situation, there could be a lot of blood. If I were to stay out at your place, you and your mother and father could be caught in a crossfire. I can't do that to you or them. The last thing I want to see are innocent victims. Kilbane doesn't care, he'll kill anybody who gets in his way. And enjoy doing it, smile and laugh and blaze away. So you see, I can't stay with you, dear, even though I'd like nothing better."

"You can at least come back with me now. Look at you, you could use five baths, one right after another."

"That I'll take you up on, if you're sure it's okay."

"Would I ask if it wasn't? And after, we can talk and have dinner and you can stay overnight."

"Maude . . ."

"Please, just one night can't be dangerous; you just got here for pity's sake!"

"Okay."

* * *

Fancy bathed for only the third time since departing Topeka, scrubbing diligently with a hard bristle brush and face cloth and Pears soap, at least one bar of which she carried with her everywhere she traveled. She freed her skin of the dust of No Man's land, the Oklahoma Panhandle, and stepped out of the battered old plunge bath, drying herself briskly. A hazy-glassed full-length mirror hung on the door. It was so old it looked on the verge of falling out of its frame and shattering on the floor. She studied her nude reflection, her long coal-black hair, her dark, luminous eyes submerged in weariness. She squared her shoulders, bringing her full, round, pink-nippled breasts high. Down their cleavage, just under her heart was a faint scar where Kilbane's bullet had struck.

Not a scar, she mused, touching it lightly with her fingertip, but a decoration for having survived the one-sided affair. Would the scar disappear the day Kilbane died? She placed her hands against her rib cage under her breasts. She filled her lungs to capacity and slowly slid her hands down the concave plane of her stomach to her sex.

Memory of Richard came sweeping back, breaking like an ocean wave, flooding her mind. She closed her eyes, fighting back the hurt. She turned from the glass, walking to the bed and dropping down onto it. She turned over. Lying face up, she stared at the ceiling, then slowly closed her eyes again.

She could smell the newly mown hay in the towering stacks. Clouds quilted the heavens, hiding the moon and stars. The air was warm and damp, threatening rain. In the woods at the edge of the field an owl hooted mournfully. They lay naked in the hay, their bodies locked, her breasts pressed hard against his chest. The familiar delicious tingling flowed downward to her sex. Moist and ready, it mutely demanded his member. He pressed it rigid, warm and throbbing against the inside of her thighs. His exploring finger found her sex, parting the lips, then gently caressing the tops of them only, igniting her clitoris. She could scarcely breathe her heart was pounding so. No words passed between them; their husky breathing and kissing were the only sounds to break the night silence.

He mounted her and thrust forward, entering. And the rain started. Fat drops fell, thumping, splashing against his back and her face and widespread legs. Her hips rose and fell, taking him into her burning sex. Suddenly the rain was descending furiously, as if the black bowl of the sky had scooped up the oceans, turned back over and was spilling them. So heavily did it rain, so loudly, she could hear nothing else, not even the sounds of his exertion. Up, up, up, she drove, abandoning all control, her head tossing, her hair drenched and sticking to her face, her eyes dimmed by the downpour, wild, wanton, wanting more and more of him, his member, his body limbs and all to dissolve and fill her sex to bursting! Driving, driving, gyrating on his erection, slamming the walls of her sex . . .

They came together, the storm at its height, the rain so heavy now it was like a huge press descending upon them. They ignored it, reaching climax a second time, his come flooding her, hers meeting it, two waves crashing together, filling her. And still she bucked, driving, driving against his erection, still as firm as a spike.

Bucking, bucking, bucking, bucking! Coming again and again until exhaustion overcame them both. He withdrew, they separated, he lay beside her. And the rain continued to batter them mercilessly. But neither reacted to it, neither uttered a sound. Lying motionless, holding hands, they let the heavens punish them, and smiled, satisfied, content.

"Dear Lord, let me find Kilbane, let us meet face to face

and have it out once and for all. Send me to burn in hell to punish me for killing when I die if you will, but give me his worthless life. Give me an eye for an eye."

She shook off the hurt and bitterness and put on her dress, ironed for her by Maude. The three Catletts and their guest sat down to roast beef, boiled potatoes and garden vegetables, the first decent meal Fancy had enjoyed since leaving Topeka. Maude's father and mother were typical farm folk, slaves to acreage and household, king and queen of the empire of their efforts, but friendly, outgoing and lavishly generous. Mrs. Catlett piled Fancy's plate with food and insisted she stay with them while in Lipscomb. She could not tell her why she could not do so, but refused her offer as politely and diplomatically as she could.

After dinner she and Maude went out to sit in the balmy night under the stars. Mrs. Catlett declined their offer to help clean up. Maude had scheduled her wedding for Saturday, one week from tomorrow.

"I haven't finished planning yet; haven't done much of anything except make my dress, reserve the church and ask the Reverend Sprague to perform the ceremony. The guests have been asked, but you see Lee and I have already bought a little place out the other end of town and I've been so busy furnishing it and just plain shopping for whatnot, I haven't gotten round to the flowers or talking to Eugenia Stembacher about playing the organ, or picking my bridesmaids, tons of details."

"Time's getting short."

Fancy gazed out over the vast, seemingly endless wheat fields stretching back from the rear of the house. Maude told her that her father and mother had been among Lipscomb's earliest settlers. Addison Catlett held the distinction of being the first to plant wheat in the area. He boasted nearly four thousand acres and had already amassed a fortune.

"He doesn't need the money, but all he does is work, work, work. We never get to go away, which is something I'd love. I'd love to go to New York and Europe and Asia. Of course, getting married, settling down I'll probably never get to go anyplace."

"What does Lee do?"

"Deputy sheriff. But he has much bigger plans. Sheriff Henry Cleghorn calls him his number one. How I love my Mr. Haverstraw! I should be ashamed the thoughts that run through my head when we're together. He can be a rascal, but I adore him. We adore each other. He's so tall and handsome and ambitious. Wait'll you meet him. He'll be big some day, I'm sure of that. Daddy has offered him a job, but he says he doesn't want to work for his father-in-law. Not that he doesn't like Daddy; they get along wonderfully, but Lee's like a lot of boys, men, they just have to do what they've set their hearts on. He eventually wants to get into politics. I do hope he turns in his badge for good one of these days. Being a deputy can be dangerous. There are all sorts of renegades and troublemakers running around Lipscomb County."

"Practically every county in the West, I'm afraid."

"What does your father do, Fancy? Is he a peace officer?"

"He was, he's dead. He was a Texas Ranger. He was killed by the Comanches. I left Texas and went to live with my aunt and uncle in Missouri."

"What about your mother?"

"She died when I was little. There was just Daddy and me till he died."

"Those guns you carry, can you really shoot them?"

Fancy smiled. "I think I can. I should be able to, I've practiced enough."

"Have you ever killed anyone?"

"On my ninth birthday Daddy took me out back. We had a little spread north of Bagwell, just below the Oklahoma line. He handed me his Navy Colt thirty-six and set an old jug on the fence and said 'Fancy, bust it.' The gun only weighed two pounds, but it felt like two hundred to skinny little me. I could barely raise the barrel. I shot six times eyes closed, naturally, and never came close. But I practiced and practiced and practiced and by the time I was ten I could hit most anything within range."

"I've shot all sorts of guns, of course. Who hasn't living out here? But I always close my eyes. I always miss by a mile. Lee kids me unmercifully. How do you keep your eyes open?"

"It took me a week to learn."

"Are you really a good shot, honest and truly?"

"I usually hit what I aim at."

"Wonderful!" She jumped up from her chair, suddenly all agog. "You must show me, I want to see."

"It's starting to get dark."

"Please, Fancy. I'll get Daddy and Mother to come watch too. You stay here, I'll get your pistol and cartridge belt." She paused. "What'll you use for a target?"

Demonstrating her skills in front of her hosts was the last thing Fancy wanted. But so taken with the idea was Maude, that she didn't have the heart to turn her down.

"Bring three parlor matches."

"I'll bring the whole box."

"Three will do."

The targets, the gun and ammunition and the rest of the audience were collected. Fancy instructed Maude to set the three matches upright, six inches apart in a crack in the top rail of the fence about forty-five feet distant. Fancy loaded and slowly raised the Peacemaker.

She fired three shots in rapid succession. One after

another, the three matches burst into flames. Everyone applauded. A second time she raised the gun, pulling off the fourth, fifth and sixth shots. One after another, the matches were extinguished, their lower ends blown cleanly off. Maude ran to the fence, Fancy and her parents following. The three match stubs were still wedged in the crack. The targets were lost in fissures in the large outcropping situated behind the fence.

The performance ended, Fancy's host and hostess said their good nights and went inside to bed. She envied them; she was so tired she had to fight to hold back yawn after yawn. But Maude wanted to talk—about her fiance, Kilbane, Lipscomb, about everything under the moon, which hung like a round, staring, disapproving, even baleful eye in the heavens.

They went to bed much too late for Fancy's liking. She slept like the dead.

Two

Sheriff Henry Cleghorn was younger than Fancy had pictured. She called on him the next morning, accompanied by Maude.

"You just missed Lee. He's on his way over to Higgins to pick up a prisoner. Fellow got drunk, shot up the local watering hole and wounded a couple of barflies."

Maude introduced Fancy. He gestured them to sit in round-backed chairs. The office smelled like undiluted ammonia, the fumes so powerful Cleghorn's eyes were watering. The two windows facing the street and the door to the empty cells in the rear were open to let the breeze carry the odor outside.

"Had a couple drunks here last night," Cleghorn explained. "Darned fools threw up all over their cell. They were sober as two deacons by eight this morning when I came in. I made 'em clean it up before I let 'em go." He grinned, showing under his reddish-blond mustache even white teeth with a lonesome-looking gold one shoved into their midst. "There heads must have been hammering to beat the band the way they were moaning and groaning while they worked. I swear strong drink is the curse of Creation. Never touch the stuff myself, not even beer."

"Sheriff," began Fancy, "I expect you're a busy man so I'll get right to the point. I'd like to hire on with you."

"As what, pray tell?"

"Deputy."

He looked from her to Maude, back to her, back to Maude, fixing her with an astonished stared. "Is she pulling my game leg?"

"She's not, Henry. She's an experienced peace officer. Tell him, Fancy. She can shoot the eye out of a turkey at two hundred yards. Tell him, Fancy. She's a miracle. She can ride, rope, and she doesn't know the meaning of the word fear!"

Fancy sighed. If Maude didn't slow down, the sheriff, already smiling, would begin laughing out loud.

"I'm afraid I do know the meaning of the word fear," she said. "Anybody who wears a badge and doesn't, shouldn't have the job."

"Amen," said the sheriff nodding, sobering, shifting his attention back to her.

Fancy got out two letters of recommendation from peace officers she had worked for, one from Sheriff Lovingtree, the law in Cheyenne Wells, Colorado, the other written by Elgin Sutter, the sheriff in Baptist Church, New Mexico. Both letters were effusive in their praise of her skills and character. Both men ended their highly favorable opinions with regrets that she had eventually found it necessary to leave their employ.

"These boys make you sound like Bat Masterson in gingham and lace," said the sheriff. He folded the letters, returned them to their respective envelopes and handed them back. "I'm impressed. Okay, you're hired."

Fancy gasped.

Maude sang, "Henry Cleghorn, you've just hired yourself one amazing deputy, able, loyal, responsible, experienced, cool under fire . . ."

"I read the letters, Maude."

"Did you say . . . ?" began Fancy haltingly.

"I said you're hired. I need another gun steady. Arnold Kimbell quit on me to go to California. All I have permanent is Leighton Haverstraw. I do have four fellows I can tap on the shoulder and draft part time if they're needed."

Once more she gulped. "Thank you, Sheriff."

"Call me Henry. Nobody calls me Sheriff, not even the little kids."

"I'm hired—"

"On one condition." He smirked, showing his gold. It snared sunlight, gleaming brightly, briefly. "One reason, really. If I don't at least give you a crack at it, Miss Tenacity Catlett here will never let up on me. And no doubt get her man, Deputy Haverstraw, to bang away at my other ear, the same time. You come highly recommended, Deputy Hatch. Let's see if you're as good as your letters say."

"I'll do my best."

He drew open a drawer, poked about, came up with a third of a chaw of plug, tossed it in the spittoon, then came up with a deputy's badge with one of the points badly bent. He straightened it.

"The pay's standard, five hundred a year plus two dollars per arrest. You get ten cents a mile to feed and fetch in prisoners, fifty cents for serving a first subpoena, thirty-seven for each one thereafter. Austin permits you to accept any rewards offered for services rendered. The county pays ammunition and one-time replacement of your firearm if it's ruined or lost in action. You'll never get rich and you may get killed. Still want the job?"

"Yes, sir."

"Henry."

"Henry."

"On your feet and raise your right hand. Do you, Miss Frances Hatch, solemnly swear to abide by the laws of Lipscomb County and the State of Texas and defend and protect the citizens of Lipscomb County and their property at the risk of your life if need be and to the utmost of your abilities?"

"I do."

"Then I hereby appoint you my deputy sheriff."

He moved to pin her badge on. He slowed his hands and stopped them an inch from her bulging breast pocket. He handed her the badge. She pinned it on.

Maude clapped Fancy on the back.

Fancy was still tempted to pinch herself to make sure it wasn't a dream. By pure chance she had come upon the one man in a hundred who treated her as his equal. She was going to like working for Sheriff Henry Cleghorn. If this sort of blind luck was to be her lot in Lipscomb, if it continued in her quest for Kilbane, she could very well find and finish him off before the week was out!

Passing thoughts of Kilbane roused her conscience. She was doing it again, accepting a star and the responsibilites that went with it under false pretenses. Her sole reason for taking the job was to cloak her search for Kilbane in legality. She hadn't said one word to Cleghorn about him; had she, he would have turned her down on the spot. Peace officers could have no part of personal vendettas.

Eventually, she would have to tell him. Tell him as well that her stay with him was only temporary, that if Kilbane was not around she would be leaving to search for him elsewhere.

"Congratulate me," said Henry to Maude, "you're

looking at a man who's just doubled his staff. Deputy Hatch?"

"Yes?"

"I'm going to give you your first assignment right here and now. It's not going to be easy, it may be distasteful, you may not like it, but it has to be done and you've got to do it."

"What?"

"Get a mop and the water bucket and find something sweet-smelling, bay rum or rose water, something, and swamp this place out. These ammonia fumes are getting to be more than flesh and blood can stand."

Three

The room in the Lipscomb House Hotel assigned her by Manager Willis was not nearly as dirty and neglected as Maude had given Fancy to believe. It was spacious; the wallpaper adorned with squares framing huge flowers of various colors was hideous, the wash basin cracked and with a large piece missing from the lip, the mirror needed polishing, but the white enamel iron bed with brass knobs boasted springs and was reasonable comfortable, and the linen was freshly laundered.

Maude had gone to church to discuss her wedding with the Reverend Sprague. It was nearing noon hour; Lipscomb sweltered under the same ruthless sun that had punished it the day before. Fancy had finished her office chore to Henry's satisfaction, had just finished changing her sweat-soggy shirt and freshening up when a knock sounded at the door.

"Who is it?"

"Leighton Haverstraw."

She opened to a man who looked nothing like the picture of him Maude had painted in her mind. He was six feet and well built but, at least to Fancy's way of thinking at first sight, not exactly handsome. His nose was too large, his lips too thin and his jaw box-shaped. But he displayed a marvelous smile.

"Fancy?" He extended his hand. She shook it.

"Come in, this is a surprise."

"Henry and Maudie told me you were checking in. I understand you two have really hit it off. She's already touting you as her best friend. And Henry's hired you on as a deputy, has he?"

He reached forth and tapped her star. The gesture surprised her and she almost shrank from it, but immediately dismissed her mild displeasure when his smile broke out again.

"Can I come in?"

"Of course."

He closed the door and looked about. "A shame you have to stay in this flea bag. A shame it's the only hotel in town. Lipscomb's not exactly Kansas City. Maudie tells me you came down from Topeka. I know the chief of police there, Orson Hill. Were you working for him?"

"No, just stopping over."

He was staring at her breasts impudently. He licked his lips. His eyes rose to her face.

"If you don't mind my saying so, not to embarrass you or anything, but you are one beautiful lady."

"I . . ."

"I haven't seen the likes of you around town since—never." He leered and up came his hands, grasping her shoulders. "Beautiful . . ."

She tensed. In a flash he was holding her tightly, his mouth clamped against hers, his tongue butting against her tightly clenched teeth. She struggled and managed to free her mouth. She pushed hard at his forearms to break his hold at the small of her back.

"What the devil do you think you're doing?" she rasped. "How dare you!"

"Beautiful. Oh, man alive. What in hell are we waiting for, lady, here's privacy, there's the bed."

She broke free and backed away from him. He continued leering at her.

"You keep your hands off me, *Mr.* Haverstraw."

"Oh, come on, Fancy, let's be friends."

"You're getting married. Very shortly; or has that slipped your mind?"

"Not for a second. And to the greatest little lady around, but that's the point, don't you see? I've only got three weeks left to kick up my heels. A bachelor's entitled to have a little fun before they put the noose around his neck. You can't argue that."

"Find somebody else to have your 'fun' with. I'm not interested."

"You trying to tell me you're a virgin, pure as the driven snow?" He laughed and slapped his knee.

"I'm not trying to tell you anything, just leave me alone. I mean it!"

"Are you engaged to something? You're not married."

"I don't believe you."

"Oh, come on, Fancy, be a sport. Let's stop jawing and strip down and have us a little romp."

"Get out of here." Marching past him to the door, she wrenched it open. "Out!"

His self-assured smile faded. "All right, okay." He started out, stopped and turned back to her. "You won't say anything about this to Maude. You wouldn't want to hurt her."

"Get out of here!"

"I'm going, but hey, we're going to be seeing a lot of each other. We're going to have to work together, we can't do it at each other's throats. You and me got to get along."

"We'll get along just fine. All you have to do is keep your hands to yourself. Get that into your skull and keep it there. *I'm not interested!*"

"You're a hothead for fair. A regular she-cat. You don't know what you're missing, lady."

"And I don't care."

She waved him out and slammed the door, bolting it. The bastard, she thought. Of all the nerve! She hadn't told him whether she'd tell Maude or wouldn't; it was just as well, let him stew over it. As if he would, as if he cared . . .

"Poor Maude."

If she had any idea what she was getting into, if she had the remotest inkling that her beloved, her hero had feet of clay and the morals of a crib-in-the-window whore, she would die of humiliation. She'd be devastated! If only there were some way to warn her, stop her before it was too late.

The disgusting pig! He ought to be horsewhipped, better yet, emasculated. The filthy-minded animal!

She stood before the wash stand mirror. "And you've got to work shoulder to shoulder with him. You've got to count on his gun as much as he counts on yours."

She shook her head despairingly. How could everything go along so smoothly and suddenly fall apart completely? Perhaps it was an omen, perhaps she was wasting her time pinning on a badge and going out hunting on the sly for Kilbane. Maybe the smartest thing she could do would be to give Henry back his star, pack up and get out. Scour the area for Kilbane, find him or not and if the latter, leave. Return to the haystack and resume her search for the needle.

Within half an hour she clamed down and dismissed Leighton Haverstraw and his antics from mind. She ate lunch alone in the Texas Flower Cafe across the street from the hotel. She was finishing her second cup of coffee when her attention was drawn to the front window. A familiar figure stood waving and smiling.

Fancy's heart sank. In sailed Maude, plumping herself down opposite.

"I've been looking for you. I went up to your room. Did Lee come up and introduce himself? He said he was going to . . ."

"Yes."

"Isn't he just a dream? Oh, Fancy, I'm the luckiest girl in the world. You do like him."

It seemed absolutely essential that she should. She nodded. "He's very nice."

"He's my Prince Charming!" She held up her hand, displaying her diamond. "And a week from today, the longest week of my life, you bet, I'll become Mrs. Leighton Haverstraw. And do you know what you're going to be, Miss Fancy Hatch? My maid of honor!"

"Maude . . ."

"Oh, yes you are."

"I couldn't."

"Why not? I'm asking you; will you be my maid of honor? I can't ask Annie Shockley. She's five hundred miles away." She covered Fancy's hand with hers. "Please say you will, Fancy, please—"

"I guess. If you're sure it's me you want."

Out came assent and triggered a feeling akin to nausea, although not in her stomach, but her heart. For her to stand beside Maude as her maid of honor, take part in the solemn ceremony of her marriage to him would be like aiding and abetting a crime! Oh, Maude, she thought, if you only knew what you're getting into. If only there were some way to tell you without hurting you.

The cafe ceiling was too low, investing the place with a seemingly permanent gloom, in sharp contrast to the dazzling brightness outside. But the food was good and nearly every table was occupied. Maude babbled on about "her Lee." Fancy listened politely and finished her coffee.

"You're done, good!" She stood up and took hold of Fancy's hand. "Come with me."

"Where to?"

"Next door to Mademoiselle Claudette's. You've got to be measured for your dress. I'd make it myself, only I don't have time. Come."

MADEMOISELLE CLAUDETTE OF BOSTON IN LISPCOMB
"Milliner to ladies with taste and pride in their attire"

The shop was resplendent with lovely clutter, as if every woman of fashion in town had descended upon it at once to poke through the merchandise. Mademoiselle Claudette emerged from the back room through a drape with a measuring tape around her neck and scissors in hand. She greeted Maude graciously in heavily accented English. She was middle-aged, short, pretty, patently dedicated to the preservation of her youth. Maude explained what was needed and Claudette set about measuring Fancy.

"Thirty-eight, twenty-four, thirty-four." She rolled her eyes suggestively. "*Tres louable!* Claudette will make you look like a princess. You, *mon cher* Maude, your bridesmaids, all of you will look *magnifique!* But Claudette is disappointed in you, Maude." She shook her finger. "You did not let her make your wedding dress!"

Maude was about to respond when the doorbell jangled and in strode Henry Cleghorn. He removed his hat and nodded greeting.

"Sorry to interrupt, ladies, but Fancy, I need you right

now. There's been a shooting out on the Ochiltree road. One of the stage passengers just arrived in town with the bad news. The stage was held up, the shotgun murdered and the driver seriously wounded. They've taken him into Ochiltree to a doctor. I want you and Leighton to get out there fast as you can ride. Some of the passengers should still be there. Question them, find out where the gundowners headed. He's waiting for you over at the stable. Check your weapons before you leave; if you get lucky, you're going to be needing them.'

The dead man had been removed with the wounded driver. Three passengers were still there when the two deputies arrived. Two of the men looked like drummers to Fancy, the third was a dusty, seedy-looking old prospector, from all appearances. Every last tooth had fled his gums and standing before Haverstraw excitedly describing the hold-up, he looked to her like a leather sack crammed with haphazardly assembled bones with his head nestling on top. Haverstraw took immediate charge of the questioning. To his credit, he had made no effort to embarrass her or himself further on the way out from town. Indeed, the incident in the hotel room appeared to have vanished his mind completely, either that or he was pretending to himself that it had never occurred. There was no way he could have forgotten it this soon. She certainly hadn't!

The stage lay on its side in the rain ditch, the left rear wheel shattered, as if it had been kicked into kindling by a horse. Three of the four horses in the team, having been freed from their traces, grazed nearby. The two drummers were dressed all but identically; she wondered, if they patronized the same tailor? The only difference she could see was that one sported a brocade vest in spite of the heat. Mr. Capehart, the vested one, peddled whiskey; his companion, Mr. Grissom, pianos and organs. Mr. Bricuse, the sackful of bones, did not divulge his line. He was too busy talking about everything else, most of it completely irrelevant. Haverstraw was obliged to raise both hands and all but threaten him to get him to shorten his answers.

"You say there were only two of them. What did they look like?"

The three agreed: the two holdup men were both young, clean shaven, probably brothers. Grisson was positive regarding the last. One had a black eye, possibly given him by the other, from the way they continually argued during the few minutes it had taken for the job. Both had ridden roan stallions.

"How many passengers?" asked Haverstraw.

"Eight," piped Bricuse. "We woulda . . ."

"When they rode off, which way did they head?"

"That way!" snapped Capehart and Bricuse, pointing in opposite directions. Grissom agreed with Capehart.

"It looked to me, and it's just my opinion," he ventured, in a voice so deep Fancy half expected a chug-a-rum to emerge to punctuate his words, "they were heading for Glazier, over the county line into Hemphill."

"That could be," said Haverstraw to Fancy. "They could board the Southern Kansas coming through Glazier and ride all the way to New Mexico. How much did they get?"

Bricuse shrugged. "Nary a plugged nickel offn' me, I'm flat busted. Poker game in the Ramrod Saloon down to Mobeetie. I swan, evvybody at that table had aces up their sleeves, cep'in' me. Course, I'm no great shakes at seven-toed Pete, nor draw neither. I . . ."

Up came Haverstraw's hands again. "Okay, okay!"

The holdup men had taken rings, watches and a total of almost $400 cash from the two drummers.

"We've got to get moving," said Haverstraw, "I'm

afraid you boys'll have to get into Ochiltree any way you can. You could take the horses and bareback it."

"What choice do we have?" asked Capehart, who to Fancy was stout and soft-looking as a pillow. He probably hadn't ridden a horse in twenty years.

She and Haverstraw mounted. "We'll catch up with 'em," he promised waving. "Check with the law in Lipscomb in a day or so. Sheriff Henry Cleghorn."

Off they galloped. Heeling the Barb, increasing the pace, Fancy came up beside him.

"They've got better than an hour's head start," she said, "what makes you think we're going to catch up with them?"

"They'll have to wait for the train in Glazier, won't they?"

"How can you be sure they're even heading there?"

"They have to be. It's a good twenty miles from here. They'll likely be sparing their mounts, so they won't be in a grand rush."

"You don't think so."

"Correct. If you want to catch a road agent, you've got to learn how he thinks."

"Is that a fact?"

"Are you sure you want to get into this? It could turn hairy awfully fast, you being a woman."

"Let's not start on that, okay? If you don't approve of my tagging along I guess I'm just out of luck."

"Forget luck, just see that you stay out of my line of fire."

"I'll try."

"Watch me, do what I do; that way you may not get yourself killed. They'll be sparing their mounts, all right. They've got no idea anybody's on their tail this early. If that stage passenger hadn't ridden one of the team into Lipscomb they'd be boarding the train before we even got out to the scene. Henry said the fellow who brought the word wired to Ochiltree to get help for the wounded driver."

"Wouldn't Ochiltree have been easier and faster for him than Lipscomb?"

"Sure. It's almost twice the distance to Lipscomb, only Ochiltree's where Henry's not. The sheriff generally locates in the county seat, or didn't anybody ever tell you that?"

"I dimly remember it."

"Good."

"Doesn't Ochiltree have a sheriff? It's the Ochiltree County seat, isn't it?"

"Ochiltree's got next to nothing. The saloon and the church are tents. I'm going to pick it up. You think you can stick close, like within a hundred yards or so?"

"I'll try."

He spurred his horse faster. She did likewise to Lady and passed him easily. They were heading southeast, down the bottom of the Great Plains, the sprawling wheat lands gradually giving way to cattle country. Across Wolf Creek they splashed, ascending the opposite bank and thundering on. There were no towns, no settlements of any size between Lipscomb and Ochiltree, nor between either and Glazier. They occasionally passed ranch houses. They rode for almost half an hour, their horses beginning to lather. Fancy, who continued to lead him, suddenly called out, pointing to her left.

"Look over there in the yard!"

Two roans were tethered to a rail fence. They stood swishing their tails, whipping away green flies. She pulled up sharply. He came up alongside. A barn painted bright red with white trimming stood about a hundred feet from the left rear corner of the house. Both doors were wide open, but the shadows prevented their seeing inside. She swung lady about.

"What are you doing?"

"Let's go back about two hundred yards or so, cut over and get behind that barn. There's no other cover here as far as I can see. Besides, we should check the barn?"

"What for?"

"Count the horses. It could tell us how many men we'll be up against."

"You check it."

He sped away; she followed his dust. Having renounced his campaign to get her into bed, he was turning to sarcasm to salve his wounded ego. They veered off the road to the right, circling wide to get behind the barn. Let him snipe, she mused. Let him let out the child inside; snide comments were preferable to having to beat him off with her fists. God forbid he should start something, forcing her to hit him. Her steel-reinforced gloves had broken a few noses and blackened a few eyes in their time. How could they possibly return to Lipscomb and convincingly explain one or the other to Maude?

She did wish she hadn't been so quick to agree to be her maid of honor. Playing sheriff's deputy was suddenly keeping her too busy to look for Kilbane, but when this piece of grief was over she would get to it, and if she failed to find him—under a rock or elsewhere—she could pull out. But not right away. She had a dress fitting and a date in church next Saturday.

They reached the far side of the barn. She pressed her ear against a bright red upright plank. There was no sound within.

"See if you can sneak around front and get a good look inside," he said. "Meanwhile, I'll get around to the side window."

"Leighton, please, let's not rush into this. Just stay here, I'll make this fast as I can."

"Woman—"

"Fancy, if you don't mind. Please stay. I really do know what I'm doing. Cross my heart."

She made her way quickly down the side of the barn out of sight of anyone in the house. Shifting the 10-gauge to her right hand, readying it for action, she eased around the corner and peered inside. Close as she was, it was still too dark to see within. The interior reeked of manure and she could hear a rat scampering. Moving slowly, she ventured inside. Her eyes quickly became accustomed to the darkness. There were four horse stalls; all were empty. She sighed relief. It made the chances good to excellent that the only two people in the house were Mr. Blackeye and his brother.

She returned to Haverstraw with the good news.

"Let's go, we'll hit them through the back door," he said, "surprise 'em. When they run out the front, we'll cut 'em down before they get within twenty feet of their horses."

"Why don't you stay right where you are? I'll get around the front." She explained her plan. It was a strategy tailored to the situation that was almost as old as time, but almost always worked.

"When they come out the back door and go for their horses, you'll have them cold."

His eyes said eloquently that he didn't want to handle it her way, but his experience or something else apparently advised him that she was right.

"Go ahead," he said, his tone begrudging. "Only try being careful. Maudie'll have fits if I bring you back slung over a saddle dripping blood in the street." He was saying it to unnerve her; her response was a smile.

She circled the barn and made it to the front of the house

as fast as she could, crouching, staying close to and under windowsills. Pressing her ear to the door, she could hear talking inside, but could not make out what was being said. They were in the rear of the house, possibly in the kitchen. She crossed her fingers that Haverstraw would have sense enough not to show himself. Slowly, carefully, she tried the door. It was locked. Backing off, she aimed the 10-gauge, blew the lock off, kicked the door wide and put two more shots inside. In the close confines of the front room they sounded like mortars. Quickly, she ran around to the side window, dropping the shotgun. She broke the glass with the muzzle of her sixgun and blasted away.

They cooperated splendidly, panicking, running for the back door. Looking out, they could see no one. Out they boiled, heading for their horses around the other side of the house. Fancy, meanwhile, reached the right rear corner and watched them. Haverstraw stepped out from behind the barn and without a word, fired his rifle. One of them had gotten to his horse and started to mount. The bullet caught him squarely in the back. The other gasped, froze and slowly raised his hands.

"Don't shoot, don't shoot, don't shoot, don't shoot . . ."

She was seething by the time she joined Haverstraw.

"What in God's name did you do that for?"

"Do what?"

"Shoot him in the back, what else!"

"Oh, that was supposed to be a warning shot. So I missed. It wasn't intentional."

"I'm sure . . ."

"He kilt Wayland deliberate!" shrilled the survivor. "You saw. Shot him square in the back, no warnin', nothin'." Down came his hands. He dropped to the ground beside the dead man. "Wayland, Wayland, oh God Almighty, oh, Jesus."

Instantly he was furious. "You fuckin' murderin' bastard!"

She watched in astonishment. Haverstraw hauled off and punched him squarely in the jaw, knocking him senseless.

"You do good work, Deputy," she said quietly, "you really know how to handle a situation."

"You talk too much, but then I have to remember you're a woman."

"How do you plan to explain this to Henry?"

"Simple. Tell him it was kill or be killed. What are you all in a lather for, you think either of these scum gave any warning to the shotgun in the holdup? Or the driver? A back shot is a safe shot, that's what I always say. And if you know what's good for you, don't go complaining to Henry about it, understand? We've got the story straight, let's keep it that way."

She nodded at the unconscious man at his feet. "He'll have a different story."

"So what? Henry's not going to take his word against his two deputies. What do you say, you going to help me pile these two pieces of garbage on their saddles and we get back to town, or are you squeamish about laying hands on a dead man."

"Death doesn't make me squeamish, Deputy."

"Good."

"Some people do."

They rode back to Lipscomb, each of them trailing a horse, Wayland over one saddle, his still unconscious brother over the other. Fancy and Haverstraw said nothing to each other, not a word until they came within sight of town.

"Guess what!" he blurted.

"Mmmm."

"I'm getting hitched this coming Saturday. I'm going to be a married man. Me and Maudie, Maudie and me, husband and wife. Isn't that something? Aren't you impressed?"

"I'm overwhelmed."

She heeled the Barb, moving ahead of him well out of conversational distance.

Four

Alfred Josiah Gantner, age eighteen, black eye, blond hair and all was settled in a cell to await the arrival of the circuit court judge. The indictment would specify murder. Fancy said nothing to anyone about Haverstraw's trigger-happiness at the ranch house. Investigation proved the house to be the property of an elderly couple, recently mysteriously vanished. Considering whom she and Haverstraw had found there it followed that whatever fate had befallen the couple it was not in their best interests. The loot from the holdup was recovered and would be returned to the passengers. Alfred Gantner—call me A. J.— strenuously and continuously insisted to the sheriff and anyone else who would listen that his brother Wayland had been "murdered in cold blood and she seed!"

Henry brought up the subject Monday morning, while Haverstraw was out of the office.

"Is he telling the truth, Fancy? What did happen?"

"What did Leighton tell you?"

"I'm asking for your version."

She shrugged. "I was at the side of the house. They ran

out the back. I didn't get to the corner until they were well out in the yard."

He smiled. "You're making the house sound like a fifty-room mansion."

"In the couple seconds it took me to get around back Leighton could have called out a warning to them as he says . . ."

"But you didn't hear any . . ."

"I was blocked by the house."

"From seeing, maybe, but you must have heard. You would have if he did call out, wouldn't you? You must have seen him shoot."

She nodded. "Only by then I was in the backyard as I say and they were out of sight around the far corner," she lied, despising herself, filled with revulsion as she did so.

"What you really mean is you don't want to disagree with Leighton." He stared at her, tugging one end of his mustache pensively. Then he took a deep breath, whooshed it out and clapped his hands on his knees. "I feel like I'm beating a dead horse. I'd better let Jedediah Bartholomew sort it out."

"Who?"

" The judge. It'll all come out in the wash, I'm sure."

She rose from her chair. "If that's all for now, I have to go over to Mademoiselle Claudette's for a fitting for Saturday."

"Oh yes, Maude's wedding. Go ahead, just check back with me later in the day. See if anything's stirring that might need your and Leighton's attention."

Nothing much "stirred" throughout the week. The temporary suspension of nefarious activity gave her time to search for Kilbane. By late afternoon Friday, she was pretty much convinced that the rumor she had picked up in Topeka was unfounded, hot air, as useful as a bottomless bucket. She remained convinced until, on her way back to town, she stopped by a house to water Lady. She got permission to from the farmer. They got to talking standing by the well. As she described Kilbane his eyes slowly assumed a gleam of recognition. He told her he was sure he had seen just such a man. Had passed him on the road coming back from Higgins, situated near the Oklahoma border to the east. Further questioning established that at the time Kilbane had been traveling with two others in the direction of Lipscomb. He had never arrived, so it seemed. In this there was nothing unusual; he could have turned off any one of a dozen side roads. But suddenly the rumor was no longer a bucket minus its bottom; he was in the area if, that is, he hadn't been just passing through. She would have to begin circle searching in earnest in the hope of finding him.

Saturday was a happy day for Maude, a lost one for Fancy. From the time she got up until late afternoon she ran about tending to all the customary details and small emergencies that arise in the hours before any wedding.

The day was glorious, not too hot and with no threat of rain. The church was packed. Maude looked radiant. Leighton, dressed to the nines, looked every inch the nervous and self-conscious bridegroom. He looked very much out of character decided Fancy. Whenever they spoke to each other it was politely, with no semblance of sarcasm on his part. But the mere sight of him swept back memory of the incident in her room and the murder of Wayland Gantner at the ranch on the Glazier road.

Eugenia Stembacher did not "play" the organ as much as she abused it. The beauty of *Oh, Promise Me* was disfigured with a flurry of sour notes. No one seemed to notice, least of all Maude, her smiling father and doting, tearful mother. Mr. Catlett gave his daughter away.

Unwittingly *threw* her away, reflected Fancy, looking on. The vows were exchanged and the rings and Maude and

Prince charming were pronounced man and wife. It was all over but the rain of rice and departure. Watching them head up the street toward their new home, Fancy's heart moved in her breast. She recalled riding with Richard to the church in Noel, he in his best suit, she in her wedding gown, clutching her bouquet. Riding to the church, never to arrive . . .

The wedding of Maude Catlett and Leighton Haverstraw was the event of Lipscomb's week. But that night an incident occurred which was to overshadow it. Sheriff Henry Cleghorn was shot and killed behind his office.

Virtually everyone in town, their numbers swollen by Saturday night visitors, arrived at the scene of the tragedy minutes after it happened. Henry had been at the Bird Cage enjoying his customary one whiskey a night at the bar in the company of Stanley Firestone, one of his parttime deputies and a close friend. Finishing their drinks, the two had left and Stanley had gone with the sheriff down the way behind the buildings to the office to check on the prisoner.

"We hadn't gone ten steps from the saloon before we heard a gun go off," said Stanley to Fancy, Leighton and a small group of the more prominent townspeople assembled in the office. Outside in front the street was filled with people, the lucky ones in the forefront pressing their faces against the windows. "They shot the lock off the back door and off the cell door, too. Freed the boy and started off, coming straight at us. It was the scariest thing I've ever seen; there must have been sixteen of them, bearing down on us. It was like coming face to face with a stampede! Henry plants his feet, pulls his sixgun and starts blasting. I threw myself to the side behind a rain barrel, expecting any second one of 'em would either ride over me and crush me to bits or shoot me dead. They passed, I rolled over and looked. They'd cut him down like a stalk of wheat and trampled him . . . oh, God, what a mess he looked."

"Did y'all see any o' theah faces?" asked the mayor, portly, distinguished-looking, his drawl rural Georgia.

"I didn't see anything," said Stanley, "except horses coming at me and the ground. I heard plenty; I thought my eardrums would burst, so many guns going off all at once . . ."

Henry's body, with virtually every bone crushed and carrying thirteen slugs, four of them in his head, was removed to Mayor Dolfuss's funeral parlor. In the presence of the small group in the office the mayor produced the sheriff's badge and turned to Leighton Haverstraw.

"Deputy, by the authawity vested in me as mayoh of Lipscomb, I heahby appoint y'all actin' sheriff."

Haverstraw beamed as the star was pinned on his pocket. Fancy did not expect to be appointed to replace Henry; she did expect Haverstraw would be. Knowing it beforehand, however, in no way diminished her disappointment. She was having a hard time working *with* the man. Working *for* him promised impossible. The mayor shook his hand, the gathering, including his wife Maude, applauded. But she looked much less pleased than did he.

"Now," continued the mayor, "ah suggest you round up a posse and go aftah those murderin' swine."

"I'm calling for volunteers," announced Haverstraw.

"No!" snapped Maude. Everyone's head turned, every eye was on her. Stanley Firestone had opened the front door presumably to echo Haverstraw's request to the crowd outside. He paused with his hand on the knob and looked back questioningly at Maude. "You can't!" she said flatly.

"Miss Catlett," began the mayor.

"*Mrs*. Haverstraw. He's my husband and this is our wedding night. And you want to send him out after a pack of killers? To get himself killed like Henry? I won't let you. Lee—"

"Take it easy, Maudie." Haverstraw took her by the shoulders, looking calmly down into her eyes. "I understand how you feel. I do, and I'm sorry, but we can't let them get away with this, don't you see? I'm sheriff now, it's my job."

"No, Lee, please—"

"I'm sorry, sweetheart, time's wasting, I've got to go."

Stanley Firestone whipped open the door and echoed the call for volunteers. Roughly thirty men raised their hands and began pushing forward.

"Yo' husband's abs'lutely right, Maude," said the mayor, placing a plump consoling hand on her shoulder. "He's got to go, he's got an obleegation to . . ."

Fancy looked on in silence. Maude was close to tears, but there was nothing she could do to stop him from leaving and, from her expression, she knew it. She shook her head, lowered it and stood aside.

"Go on then, but if you get so much as your little finger hurt . . ."

"I won't, I promise, I give you my word."

Again he held her. Her eyes lowered, she didn't see him wink and grin to the others as he spoke. He kissed her quickly and went out, followed by Firestone and Fancy.

"Good huntin'," the mayor called after them.

Five

The full moon illuminated the Ochiltree road, down which the gang had fled. Stanley Firestone had not recognized any of them with his brief glimpse, but the prisoner's face was familiar to him and many others in the posse. Fancy rode in front with Haverstraw to her left and Firestone on his other side.

She thought about Henry; the moon that was lighting the road had lit up his shiny star as brightly as the North Star in the heavens. Seeing it, the outlaws had gunned him down. They had had a full week to plan the boy's rescue and decide on the best time to attempt it, when everybody in Lipscomb was either celebrating the end of the work week or home in bed asleep. One or more of the outlaws had undoubtedly drifted into town and found out that Wayland had been killed. The news had infuriated their leader, who might even be related to the boys. The gang now had a good twenty to twenty-five minute start, but a careful combing of the countryside to the west could conceivably turn them up.

They looked for groups of horses with every house they passed, Haverstraw sending a man ahead to look inside every barn to check the number of mounts and look for telltale indications of recent hard riding. About five miles out of Lipscomb Haverstraw waved his small army—close to fifty men and one woman—to a stop.

"We'll split into three groups. Stanley, you go to the right with fifteen or so, get to the next road and keep heading the way we're going. Elmer Stockton!"

"Here!" bawled an older man, sticking up his hand.

"You boys on the left flank head out with Elmer. Look down the road to the south."

Her pride stung, Fancy seethed mildly. He could delegate responsibility to a parttime deputy and no deputy and blithely ignore her. He saw the look on her face.

"You stay with me," he said, "it'll be safer."

"For whom?"

He smirked. The groups left and right rode away. He signaled those remaining forward. On they thundered through the moonlit darkness, passing field after field of golden wheat. The road began to rise into low-hill country. They had been riding for nearly an hour, every man's eyes straining, searching, wanting and a few of them not wanting to spy their quarry. Destiny was to have it otherwise; it was the outlaws who found them.

They were between fields, the land too rocky and uneven to farm, when a flurry of gunfire came at them from the left, a hundred yards beyond. Two men tumbled from their saddles wounded, one badly in the chest. Immediately, Haverstraw called a halt; the horses milled about in confusion and sudden frenzy, the men on their backs fighting to keep control. In seconds everyone was down and running for whatever cover they could find closest, sped on their way by more firing. Haverstraw and Fancy threw themselves behind a large boulder.

He pointed. "Those two hills, the one that looks like a sombrero and the smaller one to the left of it."

"I see the flashes," said Fancy. "This is no good."

"We found them, didn't we?"

"Did we? No good. Moon or no moon, this is going to be like trying to pot ducks out of range."

"You shoot at the flash, Deputy, try."

"You do, and you may hit a hand, if it isn't fast enough pulling back." She was down on her stomach, sighting down the 10-gauge, pulling off a shot, then another. "It's no good, Sheriff. We can give and take for another twenty minutes, until we're down to our last three cartridges."

"So will they be."

"You hope. I wish . . ."

"I don't care what you wish, okay?"

"We didn't split up," she finished.

She was blaming him because she didn't like him, she thought, not because he was to blame. At the time splitting up seemed proper, it made sense. She hadn't questioned it, not even to herself. They were supposed to be on the same side; one of them should start acting like it; one should take the initiative.

"I'm sorry," she said, "splitting up was the right thing to do."

"You're damned right it was. Approval accepted. Don't worry, Stanley and Elmer'll hear the shooting and come running."

"Mmmmmm."

Again she fired; it was useless, shooting as good as in the blind, without the faintest possibility that you might hit somebody badly enough to silence their gun.

"Maybe we should try and get around behind them," he said.

"A good idea."

She could hardly disagree, having thought of it herself moments before, but hesitating to speak. He was sarcastic and a chauvinist and to get even she walked on his ego, outdoing him, outthinking him. They were a pair. He called to the men closest to them left and right. The eight left behind he instructed to pour their fire into the rocks to cover him and the others on their move. She and the remaining five followed him, keeping low and well separated, moving to their left, circling the hills. So widely, it took them five minutes to get around back. Against the sky they could see the outlaws' horses bunched and hobbled above them.

"Deputy," said Haverstraw to her, "you and me and you two boys will start up one side of their horses, the rest of you the other. And for God's sake, keep down."

Circling was a move that the outlaws had to expect. The fire she and the others had drawn dispelled any hope that they might not have been noticed. This did not make it a bad move, only one much riskier than staying put behind their boulders. She, Haverstraw and the two men with them started up the hill. They had not gone three steps before shots came winging down. Haverstraw was hit, grunting, cursing, dropping to his knees and over on his side, clutching his shoulder. One of the others was hit also, in the groin and the chest at the same time. He died screaming, rolling back down the rise like a runaway log. Fancy came up to Haverstraw, down as low as she could scrunch. Two shots whistled by; a third ripped her sleeve.

"It's deep in the shoulder," he said tightly. "It feels like a branding iron."

"Don't move your arm; don't move period. I'll keep you covered."

She positioned herself in front of him protectively. If the situation had not been so grim, she thought, she might laugh out loud. He had to be the last man in the world she would ever even dream of risking her life for, but that was precisely what she was doing. She emptied the 10-gauge and went to her sixgun. The survivor to her left and the other three on the far side threw steady fire up the hill. The outlaws answered. Shots flew by Fancy and slammed into the ground.

A human shield, she thought ruefully. Then came an unaccountable brief pause in the heavy shooting, barely four seconds long, broken by single shots. Time enough for her to catch the sound of hoofbeats approaching from the north side of the hills. The defenders heard them also. They were quickly up on their horses and pounding down onto the plain. A curtain of dust rose in their wake, climbing, smudging the moon. She holstered her gun and helped Haverstraw to his feet.

"Lean on me," she said.

"It's my arm," he said caustically. "There's nothing wrong with my legs." He softened his tone. "You saved my bacon, covering me like you did. I'm grateful, Fancy. I owe you."

It marked the first time he had called her by name out of Maude's earshot. They made their way back to their horses. The men who had remained in front of the hills had joined those chasing the fleeing outlaws. Fancy and the others standing by their horses peered after them. Shortly, all they could make out was dust.

Haverstraw was in no condition to pursue; he was bleeding badly and in considerable pain. Fancy bandaged his wound with his bandanna.

"Let's get back," he said quietly. "I've got to get it dug out right away. God in heaven, it feels like my shoulder's going to explode!"

He was clenching his teeth so tightly against the pain, she pictured them cracking, breaking. The dead man was draped over his saddle and the others, including the man earlier wounded in the chest, mounted and headed back.

The house reeked of stale liquor. It was a single spacious room with a dirt floor and furnished with a number of crudely built chairs, stools and a table at which four men sat playing poker with an ancient pack of dirty cards missing corners and liberally laced with cracks. In one corner of the room stood a breakfront filled with dishes. Food and drink lay about in crates and cartons. Cots set side by side filled the space from the end of the breakfront the length of the rear wall to the opposite corner. Front and rear windows admitted sunlight.

Fifteen men were present, without exception in need of shaving, bathing and a change of clothing. With one exception: Alfred Josiah Gantner. He stood kibitzing the game, watching the green dollars pile up in the pot. An older man gazed out the front window, leaning on his knee propped up by a stool. His unruly hair was pitch black in contrast to Alfred's; his face like the others' was stubbled, but every feature bore a distinct likeness to those of the boy. Two others present also shared the family resemblance, large, curiously innocent-looking blue eyes, aquiline noses, thin-lipped, stubborn-looking mouths, high cheekbones lowering to jaws that thrust forward challengingly.

"Here he comes," said the man at the window. "You can see it's him even quarter mile 'way, with thet flat-top hat he wears an' the way he sets his mount."

"Who, Mace?" asked the dealer, his hand holding a card frozen in mid-descent. Worry filled his eyes.

"Who, Mace!" mimicked Mace. "Ain't I tolt you ten times? I swear, Elroy, ain't nothin' gets into your haid stays thar but air!"

"The card sharper with the snake eyes," said another man, joining Mace at the window.

"Faro dealer," specified Mace.

"High time he showed," said another of the card players. "We shoulda been outta here hours ago."

"Quit bellyachin'," snapped Mace, "we'll be on our way 'fore noon." He grinned showing approximately half the normal adult complement of teeth. "Hey thar, Knowles, you ol' sheep fucker, how'd you like the way I shook thet bunch offn' our tails las' night? Warn't thet somethin'? Led 'em 'round the barn till they near bumped into theyselves! Hee hee hee hee hee . . ."

"Made sense to git outta Lipscomb City, all right," retorted Knowles.

"What you 'spect us to do, hang 'round fer the funeral?"

"I don't see why we didn't keep right on goin' . . ."

"On account us Gantners, meanin' you too, got no hankerin' to ride clear down through Texas to the damn Gulf two strides ahead o' the Texas Rangers. We're goin' home to Montana; it's got too hot here, hottern' the hinges o' hell since yestiddy night."

"You gun down the law, you'll heat up the stove evvy time," said a lean, doleful-looking man, polishing his gun with a cloth.

"I purely regret thet," said Mace sobering. "I truly does. I regret shootin' the sumabitch in the front. A. J."

"Yeah?" responded the boy.

Mace narrowed his eyes suspiciously. "You sure, swear on Maw's grave, thet thet sheriff warn't the one who shot poor Way?"

"I keep tellin' you, it was the deputy. Sheriff warn't nowheres near to the house. Tell you somethin' else, it's lucky them two didn' search 'round outside 'ahind the two-holer. They woulda' finded the two ol' folks' graves. The ground on top of 'em is sinkin'."

Mace's expression hardened. "What they shouldn'ta found was you two at the house. I oughta take my belt off an' strip hide offn' you an' him. Of all the damn fool stunts, hitting thet stage on your ownsome, 'thout my permission. You coulda' got your haid blowed off!"

"Wayland did," said Knowles.

Mace glared him into second thoughts as to further comment. A knock rattled the door. The man closest to it opened it. In strode a tall, good-looking man sporting flourishing handlebar mustaches, a railroad hat and expensive broadcloth suit. He removed his gloves and shook hands with Mace.

"Here we be, jest like I promised, Kilbane, but we ain' stayin'."

"I won't delay you but a few minutes." He cleared his throat. "Gentlemen, are there any of you who prefer not to leave? If so, I have an extremely generous proposition to offer."

Everyone began babbling at once. Mace raised his hands.

"Jest shet up an' listen!"

"Thank you, Mr. Gantner. Gentlemen, I need at least five good, reliable guns to join me in an interesting and what will eventually turn out to be most profitable business venture. Is anyone interested?"

"Speak up, any o' you int'risted in ridin' with the man you got yourselves a job o' work. You can hire on or come with us home. Us Gantners an' Cousins Elroy, Knowles, Cleland with the specs, an' Jay Harold won' be doin' no more action fer some time. We dasn't raise no ruckuses up to Whitelash; we're jest gonna' loaf an booze an' maybe a few other things." He winked and grinned broadly. "An' count our money. He hee hee hee hee."

The Odds Against Sundown

Six men offered to ride with Kilbane.

"Excellent," he said, shaking hands with each one in turn as Mace introduced them. "I promise you you won't be sorry." He laughed. "Only wealthy. Mr. Gantner?"

They stepped outside. Mace closed the door. He led his visitor around the corner of the house out of sight of those peering out the windows. Kilbane got out his billfold, extracting a $100 bill.

"As per our arrangement," he said.

Mace whipped the money free of his outstretched hand, stuffing it in his pocket.

"As per. You got yourself six good men. Only one thing."

"What's that?"

"I wouldn' start operatin' 'round these parts right outta the chute if I was you. Them boys been seed an' can be identeefied. I'd purely hate to hear they got themselves hunged fer what they done with me whilest they're workin' fer you."

"You're very loyal, you're to be commended. You know it's a pity we can't work together."

"I don' work partners with no man."

Kilbane smiled. "Nor do I." They shook hands. "A pleasure doing business with you, Mr. Gantner, I hope you enjoy your trip back. You might plan to skirt Garden City, Kansas if that's your route. I hear the local constabulary there is a band of demons. The chief is out to clean up the entire state. Now, if you'll be so kind as to send the boys out, we'll be on our way. And thanks again."

"You're welcome fer sure. Seventeen bucks a head fer two-legged cattle ain' bad. Not bad at all."

"Oh, permit me to extend my heartfelt condolences on the unfortunate death of your younger brother. I understand you shot the sheriff in reprisal."

"We shoulda' got the deputy what kilt him. They was two of 'em, one a shemale."

"A woman deputy?" Kilbane's eyes narrowed to slits as he stared. "What did she look like?"

"Don' ask me, I never seed her. A. J. knows. Talk to him."

"I shall. Interesting. Very."

Six

"You can't leave, Fancy, I won't let you!"

Fancy could see tears in Maude's eyes. The bride's new home was a lovely little four-room cottage, not yet two years old. the interior had been newly painted, and the outside, Texas rose yellow. A picket fence completely encircled the cottage and rosebushes climbed trellises at the front and sides. There was a peacefulness about the place, thought Fancy, moments after she had entered, a feeling of serenity, of sanctuary from the hectic action, brutality and bloodshed currently afflicting the surrounding area.

"It's horrible!" continued Maude, "my best friend and my husband can't stand the sight of each other."

"It's not that bad, Maude."

"It's worse! Why else would you pack up and go?"

"Kilbane's nowhere around. It's possible he was, but he's apparently left. I told you when we first met that he was the only reason I came all the way down. I never intended to stay."

"I know, but it's not Kilbane who's making you leave. Not when you haven't even covered half the county looking for him. It's this stupid friction between you and Lee. I love you both; what in the world ever happened between you to make you dislike each other so? And don't say I'm exaggerating. I've seen the way you look at each other. Talk about daggers. Have you been arguing about something?"

"What does he say?"

"Nothing, just like you. What happened? I wan't to know."

"Nothing. We just don't see eye to eye on some things."

"What things?"

She couldn't possibly tell her about the murder; besides, if she went running back to him with it he'd only deny it or offer a different version. She hated seeing her upset this way, and hurt. Hated leaving her in such a state.

"Please don't go, Fancy, I beg you."

"Maude, don't do this."

"Beg! You said that farmer whose house you stopped by the other day claimed he'd seen Kilbane. He's still here; he certainly could be. If you leave now it could be another two years before you catch up with him."

She was right and there was still another aspect to the thing that troubled Fancy. *She wouldn't be leaving as much as letting Haverstraw drive her away.* The last straw had appeared when, after the doctor had removed the slug, bandaged his shoulder, placed his arm in a sling and warned him not to use it until it stopped hurting, it apparently threw a switch in his mind. He had continued to express his gratitude for her saving his life all the way back from the shootout. Now he had forgotten her part completely and returned to his snide and sarcastic ways. In spite of the fact that he needed her now more than ever. He was righthanded and it was his left shoulder that had been hit, but the wound was deep and continuing painful. He could draw, but he could reload only with difficulty and could not possibly use a rifle.

With the notable exception of Moss Kilbane, she had never known a man she disliked so intensely.

Maude continued decrying the breach between her best friend and husband, clasping Fancy's hands tightly, as if to keep her from leaving the house, let alone Lipscomb.

"I know I call Lee my Prince Charming and all the other silly things girls call the man they love, but I know he's not perfect. I know he's dead against women deputies, but only because it's so dangerous."

"Is it less dangerous for a man?"

"I'm going to sit him down and drum some sense into him the moment he sets foot in the door. He's got to start understanding about you, how you're different. Not different peculiar, just that you've got something you're bound and determined to do and you have to wear a badge to do it."

"Don't tell him that. You'll start him asking all sorts of questions! You promised to keep Kilbane our secert. You musn't even mention his name to him."

"Oh, I won't. I wouldn't go back on my word. But I'm still going to straighten him out. You have to meet him halfway, that's only fair. Please say you'll stay, at least till the end of the month."

She had no desire whatsoever to leave the area, only the proximity-be-come-the-employ of Leighton Haverstraw. Apart from being unable to get along, having no desire to, Fancy considered him a misfit in the job. Any man wearing a badge who deliberately shoots a suspect in the back was no better than the people he chased. He was not a coward; he'd proven that at the shootout, but he wasn't very bright or imaginative when it came to strategy and he was too proud to willingly accept her suggestions. Not that she was always right, but you don't stop shooting and start arguing when lead is coming at you or about to start.

How long was he destined to be acting sheriff, she wondered? Another week, a month? It didn't really matter. Working for him was as bad as with him; it couldn't be any worse. If only he wasn't so set in his opinion of a woman's place, what she could and should do, and what not. Still, in a way he was clever, actually more like devious: he never let on to Maude how he really felt about her best friend. Probably never would, thereby saving himself the need to defend his opinion and ignite an argument.

He came in, doffing his Stetson with his free hand, the rowels of his spurs jingling merrily. A broad smile creased his face as he greeted them both. He kissed Maude like a brother on her cheek. She flung her arms around his neck.

"Careful, Maudie, I'm still sore as a boil. Deputy, I was looking for you over at the office."

"I was here."

She caught herself. There I go again, sniping back. Maude frowned at her, shaking her head almost imperceptibly. Haverstraw went on.

"Mayor Dolfuss authorized me to hire another fulltime deputy. Stanley Firestone'll be working with us. I'll probably hire Elmer Stockton, too. The whole town's still buzzing about Saturday night. Pleased as punch we shot two of them, three counting the kid out at the ranch house before. Maudie, you are looking at this week's local hero. From the way the mayor talked, don't be surprised if this job turns out permanent. What do you think of that?"

"You know what I think," responded Maude.

"Do you worry about your friend here as much as you worry about me?"

"Yes."

"She did fine the other night out at the hills." He laughed. "Didn't even get yourself killed, did you?"

Clearly, he had not told Maude that she had shielded him when he was hit, that if she hadn't he could very well have been killed. Not that she wanted credit for it, but if he retained even a particle of gratitude he would have spoken up. Poor man, he just couldn't get permission from his ego. He rambled on.

"Of course, I couldn't let her get up front with our best guns."

"I was up front," asserted Fancy, beginning to simmer.

"You were? Didn't I ask you to stay back?"

Don't fall for it, he's trying to make you look foolish, she thought; don't let him. Drop it right now.

"I have to be going, Maude."

"Won't you stay for supper?"

"I'd like to, but while there's still daylight I've got things to do. You understand."

She nodded. They said their goodbyes. She left disliking him more than ever, so intensely she was suddenly as taut as stretched wire and opening and closing her fists.

"I hope your arm falls off, you pig! Ingrate!"

Seven

Haverstraw wanted Fancy's badge. He did not demand it; he didn't even politely ask her for it, not in so many words. He couldn't, not without bringing Maude down on his head, but the flags of his disapproval continued to flutter in the breeze. His sarcasm persisted. He obviously hoped to discourage her so that she would quit, implying that she was neither needed or wanted and that he did not share Henry Cleghorn's tolerance of women, particularly those "in a man's job."

Stanley Firestone did. He treated Fancy cordially and most important of all to her, as an equal. He even defended her against Haverstraw's barbs. Stanley was about thirty-five, medium build, energetic, talkative, with jet black eyes and the olive skin of his Spanish forebears. Where the unSpanish name of Firestone had come into the family he did not say. He took his new job seriously, but his new boss less so. He had been Henry's friend; he was not Haverstraw's. They got along, they didn't dislike each other, but there was no evidence of the precious chemistry of friendship, two people with one heart, that had come to characterize Fancy's and Maude's relationship. Fancy liked Stanley because he was forthright, sincere, and did not hesitate to speak his mind. She saw him in the role of a reliable ally in her time in Lipscomb.

Orrin Sturges could never be either ally or friend. Instead of hiring Elmer Stockton as a full-time deputy, as he had mentioned he might do, Haverstraw hired an outsider. Orrin Sturges was six foot six with the strength of an ox and, as far as Fancy could see, only slightly more intelligence. He was the type of individual who reacted to others' questions with a frown, silently repeating their words to himself before responding. He was not on the job two days before Stanley nicknamed him Mr. Slow. Sturges's little green eyes gleamed like emeralds in his oatmeal-colored complexion. He boasted a luxuriant head of hair only slightly darker than A. J. Gantner's cornsilk thatch. He spoke in monosyllables, gearing up his pea brain for the effort. He was not sarcastic toward Fancy, but he enjoyed Haverstraw's snide remarks. When he wasn't laughing out loud he was generally humming, outrageously off key. Fancy wondered, but only to herself, how Haverstraw could possibly hire a stranger without recommendations from anyone, accepting *his* word for his experience and capabilities. But he did. So now they were three.

Her curiosity regarding Sturges's hiring was echoed by Maude. How in the world, she asked Fancy, could Lee hire a man he knew nothing about? Perhaps Sturges's size and strength impressed him, but if all it took to keep law and order was a physique and youth, three quarters of the law men in the territories would be out of a job. In Fancy's view, Orrin Sturges was just one more example of Lee Haverstraw's unfitness for the job. The man was as poor a judge of people as Maude, she reflected gloomily.

For its size, the Lipscomb Farmers and Merchants Bank

was probably the wealthiest bank in the twenty-six counties of north Texas. Every wheat farmer in Lipscomb County and most of those in neighboring Hemphill to the south and Ochiltree to the west banked their profits at the Farmers and Merchants. A huge Corliss safe had replaced the bank's original safe, blown and robbed two years before. The safe and three small offices in a line occupied the space in the rear behind the three tellers' cages. To the left as one entered the bank was an L-shaped area with two flat-topped desks, at which no one ever seemed to sit, at least when Fancy walked by and looked through the front window.

She had received a partial pay check which included extra money due her for travel and for the arrest at the ranch house. She went to the bank to deposit the check. She got into line behind an old man who wore a full and flourishing white beard, bib overalls and a straw hat. The bank was crowded as usual, with lines at all three cages. When the elderly man approached the teller, he laid a $20 gold double eagle on the counter and asked for paper change. It was counted out for him, he counted it and turned around. He looked at Fancy standing in line behind him, his dark eyes reflecting surprise. He then lowered his head and walked out of the bank.

She took his place at the cage, endorsed her check and opened an account. The man behind her was in a hurry and put on a wordless performance of impatience for everyone's benefit, shifting his weight from one foot to the other, sighing in exasperation, rolling his eyes, turning one way then the other, alternately thrusting his hands into and withdrawing them from his pockets. When Fancy was finished, he practically leaped into her place.

But it was not Mr. Impatience who occupied her thoughts. Outside the bank she paused and began thinking in earnest about the old man in front of her. The Wells Fargo overland stage lurched by crammed with a dozen passengers, three of them obliged to ride on the roof. The express messenger riding shotgun shared the driver's box and the four horses looked as if they had just been bathed and brushed down from ears to fetlocks. They would not look so five miles out of town, she mused, her eyes following the stage. Not if the Higgins road was as dusty as Main Street, Lipscomb.

The old man with his $20 change was nowhere in sight. Save on the screen of her imagination. Again she saw his face when he turned around. Saw his dark eyes, the surprise in them and something else. She was sure she had never seen him before, but in his eyes was the unmistakable gleam of recognition.

How could he know her and she not know him? The only man close to his age she had had any contact with since arriving in town had been Mr. Bricuse, the passenger on the stage held up by the Gantner brothers. Maude's father was at least fifteen years younger than either man.

She crossed the street, walking through the dust settling after the stage. Reaching the opposite side, she turned left and walked to her hotel. In her room she sat down on the end of the bed, her chin in her hands, her wheels whirling furiously.

It was his eyes. Definitely. He had narrowed them after reacting to the sight of her with surprise. He stood over six foot tall; he was well built, although slightly hunched over in the manner of most people his age. And he had shuffled slightly when he walked. She had noticed as he walked out the door. His beard reminded her of a Santa Claus's and could easily be just as false. She had not bothered to look closely at it; there'd been no reason to. She concentrated on his eyes, erasing his other features, his beard, his hat, everything, leaving his eyes floating in space. Surprise, recognition, narrowing. Why the latter? *Why else but to conceal the surprise and the recognition!* Only too late to do so. Eyes can betray so much in such a short time. Whoever said they were the windows of the soul might well have added the mind and heart. If you didn't like someone you might hide it behind your expression, but your eyes almost always gave you away.

Of one thing she was convinced. She may not know the man, but she knew the eyes. That was ridiculous, she thought, it made no sense. Or did it? Like something striking her totally unexpectedly, another face with the identical eyes snapped into view in her mind.

Kilbane! He was in the area. He was, and up to no good as usual. It followed as well that tipping over the bank was the "no good" he was up to. He was there because he wanted to get a look inside, establish the location of the safe and the make, a Corliss. Corliss safes were the only American make which could not be opened by drilling, by dynamite or wedges or similar tools. They were constructed with a spherical shell of cast iron several inches thick with the exterior hardened by "chilling." Their so-called ground-in door rotated concentrically with the shell and internally. The spheroid form and unusual thickness severely limited usable space inside in the standard models, but this safe was at least three times the size of any Corliss she had ever seen before. Discovering that it was a Corliss might be expected to discourage the run-of-the-mill robber, but not Kilbane. If he couldn't open it with dynamite he would no doubt resort to nitroglycerine. Better yet, hold up the bank in broad daylight, force the president, Simms Farlow, or one of his tellers to open it at gun point.

Her first tragic encounter with Kilbane had been in Enid's main street seconds after he had held up the Indian Territory bank. The time had been shortly before two in the afternoon. Daylight bank robberies were common. The presence of employees and customers assured the robbers of shields and hostages. Robbing by night did have the advantage of privacy until the explosives blew, but from then on it was get in and out before the noise drew a crowd and the law.

It all fit together as neatly as cartridges in their chambers. Deciding that it did, realizing that Kilbane was here and planning on action was good to know; what was bad was that he had recognized her. From now on he would be on the lookout for her. Knowing him as she did, as ruthless as he was she could not believe that he would come gunning for her to kill her on sight. That was not his style. He wanted her dead, no question about that, but he would first want to capture her, hold her prisoner, make her sweat, savor the situation, enjoy every minute of it before he finished her.

So he now knew she was here; what he did not know was that she had recognized him through his disguise, as clever as it was. If this gave her some kind of edge she could not pinpoint precisely what it was. It wouldn't make him any less careful and, giving the Devil his due, he was a very careful man.

She had to talk to somebody about it. Carrying it around inside was like carrying a bomb with a lit fuse. She couldn't tell Haverstraw; he had to be the last person in Lipscomb she would let in on her personal problem. She didn't dare tell Stanley, much as she liked him. She didn't know him well enough yet to trust him, not the way she trusted Maude. Would telling Maude help her in any way, other than temporarily relieving the pressure, snuffing the fuse for now? Probably not. Maude was a dear; she loved her, she would trust her with her life, but trusting her with this aspect of her problem was another matter.

She had stood at the teller's cage at least five minutes.

Small wonder Kilbane had disappeared by the time she got back outside. If only she'd had the presence of mind to follow him out immediately. But, then, how could she? She had no idea he was Kilbane at the time. And it would certainly be the last time she'd ever see him in that disguise.

She freshened up, changed her shirt and went out, running a gauntlet of stares from the loungers in the lobby, holding her breath through the cloud of tobacco smoke. As chance would have it, the first person she saw outside was none other than Stanley Firestone. As he smiled and greeted her a thought struck. There was no reason to tell him of her personal involvement with Kilbane, but she could tell him what had happened, and gild the story ever so slightly around the edges to prevent him from connecting her personally with him.

"You look like you've just seen a ghost," he said.

How perceptive, she thought. She took him by the arm out of the line of pedestrian traffic back up the steps to the verandah and down it to the end. By the time they got there he was all but bursting with curiosity. She explained. He listened, his head bowed, his expression as serious as she had ever seen it.

"He's wanted in practically every state and territory."

"Texas?"

"Probably, I don't know for certain. Does it make any difference?"

"No, I was just thinking. Henry always saved all the wanted dodgers that came in. Kept them in a drawer in his desk when he took them down. He would go through the pile the last day of the year and weed out every one left from the previous year. There was only so much room in the drawer and he figured the year-old ones had either been caught or killed. Of course that isn't always the case."

"Okay, okay, let's go over to the office and have a look."

"I was just going to get a haircut."

"Get it later, I want you there for moral support."

"I understand, Fancy. Only one thing, are you absolutely sure that old man was this Kilbane fellow?"

"Stanley, I'd recognize Moss Kilbane if he was inside a grizzly."

"There's hundreds of bad guys floating around; how come you know so much about him in particular? How come you're so interested in him?"

"He shot up my home town and killed a close friend."

"Is that a fact? Where's home?"

"Noel, Missouri."

"Oh hey, I've been there. Garfield County. Had a friend used to work in the lumber mill there. Ever bump into an Otis Swenson?"

"No, come on, let's get over there."

"I'm coming, I'm coming."

Haverstraw and Orrin Sturges were sitting in the office with their feet up, passing the time of day. Stanley went straight to the desk drawer. He set the stack of dodgers on top and Fancy started going through them.

"Who you looking for?" asked Haverstraw.

"Suspect," said Fancy.

"Who?"

"Calls himself Moss Kilbane, but he uses aliases and disguises. He's wanted for murder and bank robbery. Wanted for just about everything in the book."

"Who wants him?"

She paused in her leafing and stared at him.

"The law. All over."

"She just spotted him in the bank," said Stanley.

Haverstraw shot to his feet, rattling his chair, all but upending it. "Let's go get him."

Stanley shook his head. "Relax, he's long gone. He came in disguised as an old man."

As the conversation went on Sturges looked from one speaker to the next, his mouth agape, his feet still hoisted onto a chair, his sixgun in his lap. He had been cleaning the chambers and barrel.

"If he was in disguise, how'd you know it was him?" Haverstraw asked Fancy.

"She recognized him by his eyes," said Stanley.

Haverstraw chuckled derisively. "Is that a fact."

"That's a fact," she said, stifling the impulse to snap back. "It was him all right."

"How come you didn't arrest him on the spot? At least tail him? A good deputy thinks on his feet, you know; it's what you call initiative."

"Is that what they call it?" asked Stanley, pretending enlightenment. "She would have collared him, only she didn't recollect who he was until he'd left town."

Fancy sighed to herself. Stanley was trying his best to support her, but he was starting to fumble badly and inadvertently making her look incompetent. Haverstraw was staring at her.

"You really think he's planning to rob the bank?"

"I do. If he's robbed one, he's robbed fifty. Knowing him, he's not about to pass up a plum as fat as the Farmers and Merchants."

"Knowing him? You know him?"

"His reputation. He robbed a bank in Baptist Church, New Mexico when I was working there. Tried to. We took prisoners. He attacked the town, freed his men, killed a deputy, nearly killed the sheriff. I've seen him face to face, I'd recognize him."

Haverstraw and Sturges exchanged glances.

"One of us should hang around the bank, keep our eyes open. You know what this . . . What's his name?"

"Kilbane."

"Looks like. Why don't you sort of stand guard?"

"You mean all day, every day?"

"We should take shifts," suggested Stanley, lighting a cheroot with a kitchen match scraped up the seat of his trousers. "The bank is open from eight to five Monday through Friday, till noon Saturdays. How's about taking shifts?"

"The three of us don't know what he looks like," said Haverstraw.

"We will if we find him in this pile. Fancy here'll find him and then, if we're real nice and gentlemanly, I'm sure she'll show us his pretty picture."

"You're funny, Stanley," said Haverstraw.

Fancy laughed. "I think he is."

Gloom supplanted her light-hearted mood when Kilbane's dodger failed to turn up. She described him to them.

"I think we can safely assume that he's sacrificed his handlebar mustaches. Or maybe not. He was wearing a phoney beard with a short mustache, both ends connecting to it. He could easily have hidden his handlebars under it."

"Could he?" asked Haverstraw.

"I've seen him four different times; never without his handlebars. He seems to be very vain about them. My guess is he's still wearing them."

"Can't be too many men hereabouts wear handlebars," averred Stanley.

Sturges nodded. Haverstraw watched him do so, leaving him little choice but to agree.

"Okay," he said, "here's how we'll work it. The nine hours the bank is open each day we'll split into three shifts.

It's now close to two. Stanley, you'll take the rest of today, the same time tomorrow and so on."

"Hold on a second, I was on my way to get a haircut."

"Get it cut tomorrow morning. Orrin, you can take the eight to eleven shift." He looked at Fancy. "Deputy, you'll take eleven to two. Every three days you can switch around. Work it out among yourselves."

"What are you going to be doing, Leighton?" asked Stanley pointedly.

"Tending to business, what do you think? There's other things going on around here or about to start up besides robbing the bank, which may never happen."

"It'll happen, all right," said Fancy, realizing as she said it she was sticking her neck out, but not in the least caring.

"Not if this Kilbane recognized you," said Haverstraw. "Wearing a badge. He ought to know he's wanted. If I was and I spotted a peace officer who knew me I'd get out of town and stay out."

"You could be right about that, Leighton," said Stanley, looking at Fancy as he spoke.

He very well could be, she thought, and probably was, were it anyone but Kilbane.

"He'll be back," she said confidently, "with his gang and his guns. He's in this area, he knows the bank by reputation, how wealthy it is. He came here to rob it and he's not going to leave until he tries to."

"We'll see," said Haverstraw. "How about taking another look through that stack. You may have missed him."

Stanley and she doublechecked the dodgers, but Kilbane was not among them.

"How do we watch the bank?" she asked, restoring the stack to the desk drawer. "Where do we station ourselves to keep an eye on it?"

"One of the offices in the back," said Haverstraw. "You stay inside with the door closed, out of sight of them if they should show up. You'll be able to hear everything going on out front."

Stanley shook his head. "That's no good, Leighton. What do we do when they walk in, jump out and get the drop on 'em? What if they start shooting, with the help and all the customers in the line of fire. No sir, we've got to nab 'em *before* they get inside."

"He's right," said Fancy. "Aren't there rooms up over the Bird Cage across from the bank?"

"They're occupied," said Haverstraw, turning his attention to his wound, repositioning his sling more comfortably.

"But couldn't we make some sort of arrangement with one of the people whose room overlooks the street? Post ourselves at the window. Whoever's living there must work. They'll be away from eight to five."

Haverstraw pointed out that whoever they approached would either have to be told what was going on or given some trumped-up story. And either way would have to be sworn to secrecy. The plan was beginning to unravel. Upstairs was discarded in favor of the alley alongside the Bird Cage. Still, wherever they watched from, the plan was predicated on the assumption that Kilbane, confronted by the impregnable Corliss safe, would strike during business hours, so that somebody could open the safe for him. The assumption was entirely logical.

Unfortunately, it was also wrong.

Eight

His hand caressed her breast warmly, then glided up to and around her neck, bringing her mouth against his in a passionate kiss. And while they kissed, his hand went back down to her sex. He began gently playing with her, caressing it, rubbing up and down lightly. She spread her legs, accepting his finger as it stroked her lips, bringing moistness to them, relaxing and opening them, exciting, stimulating them, exploring within, arousing her so she trembled in wild anticipation. It was glorious, she was coming, coming.

The pounding on the door was like a sledge, the sound reaching her brain, wrenching her awake and sitting bolt upright.

"Deputy! Deputy! Come quick! They're robbin' the bank! Quick!"

And whoever it was was gone, the muffled sound of steps retreating down the stairs. She threw on her clothes, buckled on her sixgun, toed into her boots and snatched up the 10-gauge. She fled the room, dashing through the lobby, blinking away the lingering cobwebs woven by sleep. She could hear shooting in the street. Down the front steps she bounded, running up the street, shots from the bank whistling past her. She came upon Haverstraw and Stanley Firestone pouring lead at the bank from the alley alongside the Bird Cage. Orrin Sturges came running up from behind them, flopping down, firing as he landed. The front window was completely shattered.

"There's four of them," said Haverstraw, pausing to reload his rifle, disregarding his wounded shoulder. He grit his teeth against the pain, wincing, glowering. He pointed up the way. Four horses were tied to the hitch rack in front of Mademoiselle Claudette's two doors from the bank.

"This is a Mexican stand-off," observed Fancy.

Haverstraw bristled. "What are we supposed to do, rush them? Run across the street, expose ourselves. They'd cut us down before we got ten feet!"

"We keep this up and pretty soon that front door is going to look like a honeycomb," she said mildly.

"Got any ideas, Fancy?" asked Stanley.

"Fancy's always got an idea," snapped Haverstraw, "didn't you know that? She's brimming with ideas."

"Is there a back door?" she asked, addressing Stanley.

He shook his head. Haverstraw tried to resume speaking, but she cut in. The left front door stood three-quarters open.

"I'm going to try to get to that door from the other side. If you can keep them occupied maybe I can get close enough to put a couple shots inside, yell to them, give them a chance to give up."

Haverstraw scowled. "Give your shotgun to Stanley there, let him do it."

"I can handle it," she said firmly.

"Let her try, Leighton, what have we got to lose? She's right about a stand-off. Go ahead, Fancy."

Haverstraw bristled. "I'm giving the orders here, Stanley, if it's all the same to you." A shot sang by his ear; he ducked instinctively. "Go ahead, Deputy."

"Thank you, Sheriff."

She ran back down the alley and behind the buildings, turning up another alley, this one barely thirty inches wide. Reaching the front of it, she paused to check the 10-gauge. It was fully loaded. People were beginning to emerge from buildings up and down the street, standing and watching the battle from behind whatever they could find for concealment. Fancy dashed across the street and staying close to the buildings, made her way to the near corner of the bank. She flattened against the wall and raised her weapon, signaling Haverstraw and the others.

They stopped firing. Her back to the wall, she eased around the corner. She shoved the shotgun through the open door and fired three quick shots, fanning them out as best she could. And swinging back out of the line of answering fire.

"Give it up! she yelled. "Drop your guns and your belts. Get your hands up and come out together."

"Come in an' git us!" snarled a voice within.

"Don't be stupid. You've seen the safe. You can't blow it, you can't wedge it open. You want to die for nothing, then stay there. You've got ten seconds to make up your minds."

There was a long, trenchant pause. Up the street and down she would hear muffled babbling, but inside the bank was as silent as the tomb. Then, straining her ears, she heard whispering.

"Last chance!" she exclaimed.

"All right, all right, all right, we're comin' out. Don' shoot! We ain't tryin' no tricks, nothin', I swear!"

Out shuffled the four of them, hands high and unarmed. Her heart high in her chest sunk like a rock. Not one of them was Kilbane. But no sooner had the last one appeared then two shots rang out, coming from the head of the alley across the way. The man in the forefront grunted, dropped to his knees and fell on his face dead.

"Damn!"

She sprang in front of them protectingly, waving the shotgun at Haverstraw and the others. They came running toward her. The three captives stood goggled-eyed with fear, shaking in their boots, their hands still upraised.

"Why did you have to shoot him?" rasped Fancy.

"Didn't mean to," said Sturges. "My finger slipped."

Her eyes shifted to Haverstraw. He was smiling. Two of a kind, she thought. Haverstraw did not even trouble himself to comment on Sturges's "accident."

"Good work, Deputy," he said to Fancy.

Like a wave rising to its height before it breaks, abject disgust with him, with Sturges, Lipscomb and all else associated with the responsibilities of her badge surged upward within. Discovering that Kilbane was not one of the four was the final straw. But then, how could she expect him to be. He would never attempt to break open a Corliss safe; he was too experienced, too intelligent. These four had not even taken the trouble to investigate the bank; dimwits that they were, they had come barreling in without any preparation whatsoever.

Two onlookers volunteered to removed the dead man to the funeral parlor. The other three, one of them Alfred Gantner, were locked up in separate cells. All four were Gantners. The youngest, Alfred, was almost eager to tell their story. Fancy questioned him. He told her that they had changed their minds about returning home to Montana, deciding to stay and pull one last job. Definitely the last for brother Arlo! And the same for Alfred and brothers Dewey and Hollis for a long time to come.

Alfred glanced about. "This here is the same cell you gimme 'afore."

Outside in the office Haverstraw overheard. "It's your cell, boy," he said laughing. "We're going to get a brass plate with your name on it."

Alfred's face hardened. "Murderin' scum. He kilt Wayland; you seed him!"

She did not want to get into discussion of that, or even of brother Arlo's murder, which was the only word to describe it. An idea came to mind, a hunch.

"Tell me something, Alfred, straight answer. The better you cooperate the easier it'll be."

He gulped, his eyes becoming huge. "They gonna hang me?"

"We'll do our best," called Haverstraw from outside.

Fancy got up and closed the office door.

"Alfred," she said, returning to him. "You and your family have been raising Cain hereabouts for months, right?"

"Not no more."

"Not no more." Her eyes riveted to his she described Kilbane. Looking as she did so for a telltale glimmer of recognition. "Have you run into him? His name is Moss Kilbane."

Alfred bunched his mouth and crinkled his forehead, plunging deep into thought. Slowly he shook his head.

"Don't know him."

"You don't."

She had seen the glimmer. It was all she needed. It was difficult to understand his willingness to tell all about his family, then turn completely around and lie about knowing Kilbane. Did he have something on the boy; was he holding something over his head? She stood up. Press him on it, she thought, here, now, and hard.

"You know him all right. Where is he? What's he up to?"

"I dasn't."

"Where did you meet him? Tell me everything."

"I'm tellin' you I dasn't. He's . . . he's diff'runt. Hard like a rock. Iffn' I said two words 'bout him an' it got back to him he'd come after me an' cut me down so quick. I know I'm goin' to the pennytenchary, but even inside thar I wouldn' be safe nohow. Not from him. He's hard, he's smart, he's got ways. You know Jake Webber?"

She shook her head.

"He was ridin' with us Gantners, him an' some frien's, all good ol' boys. He's Texas, so he didn't wan' to go up to home in Whiplash nohow. When Mr. Kilbane comed 'round askin' for men, Jake was one joined up with him. I seed Jake this mornin'. He tol' me that Mr. Kilbane comed right out an' said to him an' the others, the one thing he wanted from 'em, aside their followin' orders an' doin' things his way an' right 'thout messin' up, was . . . was . . ."

"Loyalty?"

"That's it! That's what Jake said. Mr. Kilbane is hard rock on bein' loyal. No double-crossin', no holdin' back on taking's, no under the table doin's. Jake swears he'd gun his bes' friend' down, even his onliest brother to keep things his way, protect hisself. Jake says he's the easiest killin' man ever bornded. That's what he said."

"Where did he tell you they were holed up?"

"Didn'. Cross my heart, hope to die."

"Is he planning to stick with Kilbane?"

"I think he's too scairt to leave. It's Mr. Kilbane's eyes, you know. They look right through a body. He looked inside my head when I talked to him. He's sure 'nough a man you don' dare lie to."

"What did you talk about?"

"I dasn't say."

"I'll let you in on a little secret. I'm going to collar Mr. Kilbane, eyes and all, and when I do I'll toss him right into this cell. You'll be together, if you don't tell me what I want to know."

What he told her was not exactly what she "wanted to know," although what he said didn't really change anything. He admitted he had described her to Kilbane. Since he had already seen her in the bank, it didn't mean much.

"One last question, Alfred, does he still wear his handlebar mustaches?"

"Yup, an' very han'some, too. I wisht I could grow me a mustache."

"You will. A beard too if you like."

"How long will I have to be in the pennytenchary?"

"A long beard, I'm afraid, a very long beard."

Two days later Mayor Dolfuss relieved Leighton Haverstraw of the job of acting sheriff. He appointed him sheriff. The Citizens Committee for the Improvement of Lipscomb presented Sheriff Haverstraw with a shiny new Winchester .44-.40, complete with extra sight mounted at the front of the stock. Affixed to the stock was a brass plate carrying an inscription:

Presented to

Sheriff Leighton Haverstraw
by the grateful citizens of
Lipscomb, Texas, in recognition of his outstanding service to the community

So lengthy was the commendation, no room was left on the plate for the date. The sheriff did not seem to mind. Despite her reservations regarding his choice of careers,

Maude was very proud. Stanley Firestone was very upset. He complained privately to Fancy. He reminded her that she was the one who had turned the tables on the Gantners. If they had left the decision to Leighton they would probably still be in the alley, holding up their end of the stand-off. Fancy did not disagree, but it didn't bother her as it bothered Stanley. She couldn't care less. Her mind was filled with other things.

Nine

The Gantners' unexpected visit did not alter the original plan. Fancy, Stanley, and Orrin Sturges continued to divide daylight lookout duty. Fancy was convinced that Kilbane would attempt to rob the bank, and knowing him as she did, once he made up his mind nothing would change it.

Maude mounted her husband's gift from the town above the fireplace. She dusted it and polished the engraved brass plate twice a day. Fancy visited her often. For some reason she could not put her finger on, Maude had gotten a firm grasp on the idea that her husband and her best friend had dropped the animosity between them and were now getting along. In Fancy's heart she knew that the opposite was the case, that if anything she despised Leighton more now than before the shootout. Everybody in Lipscomb assumed that it was he who had devised the strategy which had turned a stand-off into triumph. He said nothing to change the public's thinking. But from that night forward he began treating her differently, jettisoning his sarcasm, speaking to her as if he had changed his opinion and was now considering her on equal terms, or at least the same terms as Stanley and Sturges.

Fancy knew why; he wasn't stupid. He needed her as much or more than either of the other two. She had proved her worth three times under fire. He may not have liked that, it may have surprised him, but he could no longer ignore it. She did not impress him to the point where he looked upon her as a friend, but he no longer talked down to her.

She had given up her search for Kilbane; he would come to her. Nine long, boring days followed the Gantners' abortive robbery attempt. The circuit court judge was not due to arrive in town until the end of the month, nearly two weeks hence. Shortly before eleven in the morning, Fancy was on her way to the alley to take over for Stanley, crossing the hotel lobby when all hell broke loose in the street. Rushing out to the cover of the horse trough in front of Sheppard's Variety Emporium next door, she flopped down, aimed the 10-gauge at the door and was about to pull the trigger when she paused. There were innocent people inside. She could not see anybody through the partially opened doors, but they had to be there. There was no way she could shoot.

"Damn!"

Up and down the street people ran for cover. The driver of a hay wagon swiveled on his seat and jumped into his hay, burrowing to the bottom of it. She caught a glimpse of Haverstraw, who had discarded his sling, and Sturges, the two of them also down behind a trough.

Blazing away!

A woman appeared in the doorway. Behind her, his face concealed by a bandanna, stood a man holding his sixgun to her head. Haverstraw and Sturges stopped firing. The rest of the gang appeared, each one using a customer as a shield.

She recognized Kilbane by his clothing, the next to the last to show. They sidled in a line to the left-hand corner of the bank, backing down the alley. Each of them carried a bulging flour sack. Not one uttered a sound, nor did any of their shields. No more three seconds after the last man and his shield disappeared into the alley Fancy heard hoofbeats. The customers reappeared, some staggering, one woman dropping in a faint. Fancy threw a look up the street. Haverstraw and Sturges were running for their horses at the hitch rack in front of the office. She started after them. She was passing the alley across from the bank when she glanced to her left. Stanley lay in a pool of blood, gun in hand, as still as a stone. She ran to him stooping, pressing her ear to his back.

He was still alive. Barely. Meanwhile, people were emerging from hiding. She ran up to a well-dressed middle-aged couple, their faces drawn with fear.

"A deputy's been shot. Get a doctor! Quick!"

Dr. Hume, who had treated Haverstraw's shoulder wound, was summoned. Fancy stood beside him, nerves knotted and heart thumping, watching him examine Stanley.

"Two bullets in the back," he said. He was very old, painfully thin, with hands like claws and skin as yellow as a chicken's.

"Will he make it?"

"Possibly. If I can get him through the next two hours. I hate to do it, but I'll have to move him. Get him over to my place."

A litter was brought. Fancy, meanwhile, collected a dozen volunteers forming a posse. She led them out of town toward the Higgins Road, the direction taken by Haverstraw and Sturges. The all but treeless land of the High Plains undulated slightly across the Panhandle. Wildlife, apart from jackrabbits and the mice infesting the wheat fields, was all but nonexistent. The red soil gave life to wildly spreading bluebonnets, mountain pinks cloaking the hillsides, sunflowers along the roads, daisies patching the prairie like melting snow. But virtually all the color was gone by July, as the blossoms succumbed to the relentless heat.

They rode for fifteen minutes; there was no sign of Haverstraw and Sturges, let alone the outlaws. There were a dozen places where they could have deserted the road, cutting southward toward Glazier or in the opposite direction, toward Follett. Still, all alternatives considered, Fancy remained convinced that they would head for the Oklahoma border somewhere between Higgins and Wolf Creek. The question was where? The distance between the two was better than ten miles.

Overhead the skies darkened. An eerie stillness seized the air signaling an impending storm. It came swiftly, the sun vanishing, the clouds becoming blue black, lightning scratching jaggedly followed by thunder rumbling like a bowling ball down an alley. The heavens opened, down came the rain in sheets. A large, shallow sink to their right ahead began filling almost immediately, so heavy was the downpour. Elmer Stockton came up alongside Fancy.

"We'll never find 'em in this, Deputy," he said, lifting his reedy voice above the sound of the storm. "It's a regular goose drowner."

She nodded. He was right, it was useless. They swung about and headed back to town.

Two days later Haverstraw and Sturges till hadn't returned. The townspeople were convinced that they were still tracking the outlaws. Maude was certain of it. Fancy had no reason to doubt it, but one thing troubled her, something everybody else took pains to overlook.

How could Kilbane know about the lookout? Stanley had been shot in the back. He had remained conscious just long enough to draw, but he had not fired his gun. Obviously, either someone was in cahoots with Kilbane or one of his own was responsible.

But how had they known Stanley was posted there? Nobody in town knew about the daylight vigil. Had they, not one would have set foot in the bank. Nobody would have gone within twenty-five yards of the place. Not even Maude knew.

Interesting, she thought, as she left the office and set out across the street diagonally to Dr. Hume's office on the ground floor next door to Mademoiselle Claudette's. The rain persisted. Now well into its second day it was threatening to last all week. There was no sign of a break in the clouds, no slowing of the downpour. The street was a quagmire. She stepped in one hole almost up to the top of her boot, pulling it free with a loud sucking sound. Arriving at the doctor's, she found Stanley awake, lying on his stomach as usual. He looked to be as weak as water, but managed his familiar smile. Mayor Dolfuss was visiting him. The doctor had stepped out.

Fancy had never seen a doctor's office so orderly and neat. A place for everything and everything there, including pasteboard cartons of gauze stacked to a height of nine units, four abreast on the upper shelf of one of three gleaming, enameled, glass-doored cabinets. Mayor Dolfuss greeted her smiling.

"He's gonna be right as rain, so Doc Hume says . . ."

"Please don't use that word."

He laughed. She picked up the folded cloth lying near Stanley's pillow and wiped the perspiration from his forehead.

"Painful?"

"Sore. I'll be lying on my belly the next six years at least. It's fun. Fancy, don't ask me again if I saw who did it, I didn't see anything except the bank going soft before my eyes, all wavy, everything turning gray, then black."

"Deputy," interrupted the mayor, "with the sheriff and Deputy Stuhges away, you the only one left to take chahge. I theahfoh appoint you actin' sheriff until such time as Sheriff Havahstraw retuhns." He paused and stared anxiously. "You don't think he nevah will, do you?"

"I have no idea, Mayor."

"Judas priest, I hope he does! Good man, Leighton, I'm suhprised I didn't notice it befoah. I guess he's the modest type, keeps his light undah the proverbial bushel, eh?"

Disgust masked Stanley's face. "Mayor, there's a couple things you may not know. Fancy here saved Leighton's hide in that fracas after Henry got killed."

"I know that."

"Do you also know that it was her idea to take the action to those Gantners? Leighton didn't think of it. She did, and she volunteered to go to the door. He was against it."

"Stanley," she said, "forget about it."

"If that's the case," began the mayor.

"That's the case, all right!" snapped Stanley.

"Then all the moah reason foh mah appointin' you actin' sheriff, Miss . . . what's you'h last name again?"

"Masterson," said Stanley, "Bat Masterson."

"Hatch," she said.

"I'm puttin' you in chahge. Considah it done. Stanley, I have a meetin' I got to get to. I'll see y'all. Get you'hself well fast as you can, y'heah?"

"I'll do my best."

Mayor Dolfuss touched his hat, bowed slightly and left.

"Fat slob," muttered Stanley.

The Odds Against Sundown

Fancy laughed. "Tell me something, Stanley. What do you think's happened to those two?"

"Still chasing Kilbane, I guess."

"I guess."

He eyed her questioningly. "What's bothering you?"

She told him of her suspicion. He chewed on her words in silence for fully a minute, his cheek resting against his pillow, his single visible eye narrowing.

"No," he said flatly.

She shrugged. "You know them better than I do . . ."

"I don't know Sturges. As for Leighton, he may not be as spotless as Maude and everybody else in town thinks, but he wouldn't throw in with somebody like Kilbane. Sturges is another matter. Nobody knows anything about him, except Leighton, and all he knows is what Sturges told him. I'm not all that fond of him, but that doesn't count for anything."

"Stanley, they're together out there someplace. Ever since Leighton hired him they've been practically inseparable. He spends more of his free time with Sturges than he does with Maude. And they haven't even been married a month!"

"What you're saying is Sturges got Leighton's ear and sold him a bill o' goods on hitting the owlhoot trail with him. Joining up with Kilbane. Fancy, I know you don't like Leighton. You've got good reasons not to, but aren't you jumping to conclusions?"

"I'm not thinking of him, I'm thinking of both of them. As a team. That's the way they've been operating."

"They could both be lying dead in a ditch. Kilbane could have outfoxed them, doubled back, bushwhacked them, taken them prisoners. He could be holding them as hostages."

"What does he need with hostages? He got away clean. I didn't even get a shot off."

"It's only been two days. I think Leighton and Sturges will come back. Maybe not for three or four days, maybe longer than that, but they'll show up."

"I'll bet you a dollar they don't."

"You're on."

Three more days went by with no sign of either. Fancy visited Stanley mornings and afternoons, but did not bring the subject up a second time. Neither did he. Until the afternoon of the fourth day, the sixth since the holdup. Dr. Hume was out front in his office on the other side of the drape. Eyeing the drape, she lowered her voice.

"Stanley, I'm going out looking."

"I wouldn't do that. You're the only one left. You can't leave the town unprotected."

"I've deputized Elmer Stockton and two others. Temporaries. Like I am sheriff."

"Makes no difference. Somebody's got to be here to tell them what to do. You've got to stay. You're stuck."

The discussion ended abruptly as Dr. Hume came in.

"Time to change your dressing, Stanley."

Fancy left. Outside in the street she stood mulling over Stanley's words. He was right, she conceded, but sitting around waiting for Haverstraw and Sturges to return was starting to get to her. She was convinced that neither would ever show. It did seem far-fetched that Haverstraw would desert Maude. She was worried about him and becoming more so with every passing day. She insisted he was dead. She had already reached a point where she couldn't stand being in the cottage alone and had gone back to live with her parents until he either showed up or word arrived as to what had happened to him. Fancy tried her best to dissuade her from thinking the worst, but had little success.

It rained on and off until Saturday. Less than ten minutes after the sun reappeared a telegram arrived addressed to Sheriff Haverstraw. Fancy signed for it and out on the sidewalk, out of sight of the clerk, tore open the envelope.

SHERIFF HAVERSTRAW

EXPRESS OFFICE CANADIAN ROBBED OF SOUTHERN KANSAS RR PAYROLL STOP SEND AS MANY MEN AS YOU CAN SPARE TO ASSIST SEARCH OUTLAWS

C WHITTLESEY
SHERIFF HEMPHILL COUNTY

"Kilbane," she murmured.

Ten

Standing outside the Western Union office telegram in hand, Fancy decided to go "by the book," that time-worn tome invisible to the naked eye and reposing in the minds of those in authority to whom rules and regulations are sacred. In this instance the authority being the mayor. Much as she wanted to mount up and get to Higgins as fast as Lady could carry her, she could not. Elmer Stockton would have to take over as acting sheriff. Or was it acting acting sheriff? She would have to deputize at least one more man.

Or would she? There must be a U.S. Marshal's office somewhere in north Texas, possibly as near as Amarillo. It lay to the southwest less than four hours by rail from nearby Higgins. A deputy U.S. marshal sitting in Henry Cleghorn's chair for as long as it took to clean things up would guarantee a peaceful night's sleep for everybody in town. If she couldn't get a marshal there was always the Texas Rangers. True, they were based in San Antonio five hundred miles to the south, but they covered the entire state.

Standing mulling over the situation, her train of thought was suddenly derailed by a familiar voice.

"Fancy!"

Maude approached, perched on the seat of her buggy. She wore a dress of gleaming black silk trimmed with ruffles. From thirty feet away it looked like mourning. Fancy's heart sank at the sight of her. She obviously had not slept in days, kept awake by crying, her face pasty, her eyes red-rimmed. She pulled up in front of her.

"Maude . . ."

"Don't say it, I know I look an absolute fright. I should wear a flour sack over my head. Have you heard anything?" Fancy had folded the telegram; she slipped it into her pocket. "What's that?"

"Nothing to do with Leighton, I'm afraid." She approached her, placing a comforting hand on her arm. "Dear, he'll come back, both of them will."

"He's dead. I know it. I feel it."

"He's not."

"He is. Last night I fell asleep terribly late; I had a nightmare. I saw a man lying in a ditch face down. I saw myself coming up to him. I touched his back. I was afraid to look at his face. But I did; it was Leighton smiling, dead. Fancy, I went wild. I beat my fists against the ground till they bled. I woke up . . ."

"You're just torturing yourself, Maude."

"I can't help it. My intuition is good, it's always been. I trust it and I *feel* he's dead. Oh, dear God."

She buried her face in her hands and began sobbing softly. Passersby stared. Fancy got up on the seat beside her, taking the reins, winding them around the brake. She put her arm around her and held her close, patting her gently. "He's alive, Maude. If anything has happened we'd get word."

"You're wrong! It's the other way around. If he *was* alive I'd hear. He'd send me a telegram, a note, something. It's been almost a week. I'm out of my mind with worry. I can't sleep, I can't eat. All I do is pace the floor. I'm afraid to go near the cottage. Without him there it's as empty as an old barn. If I did go back I'd only sit facing the door, straining my ears for the sound of his step, praying he'll come home, the door will open and there he'll be. Oh, Fancy, Fancy, what am I going to do?"

"Listen to me, I'm going out to look for them. I'll find them. I promise I won't come back till I do."

She had no sooner uttered the words then misgivings assailed her. She had no earthly right to make such a promise. No right to promise her anything. He could very well be dead and buried God knew where. She could go on like this, waiting, hoping in vain, living on tenterhooks for months and never see him again. If he was still alive and couldn't be bothered contacting her, if he had put the effort at the bottom of his list of priorities and she did find him she would . . .

"Fancy." Maude's voice changed dramatically, losing the sobbing undertone, hardening. "Why have you waited until now to go out looking? It's been a living hell for me."

"I know. But I couldn't leave. There'd be nobody left to mind the store, don't you see?" she lied. And having done so, expanded on it. "I had to talk Elmer Stockton and another man into taking on the job of fulltime deputy. I talked until I was hoarse before I got them to agree. They have to give up their jobs."

"When are you leaving?"

"Soon as I can."

"What does that mean, today, tomorrow?"

"Today, hopefully."

"Hopefully?"

"I have to talk to the mayor, get his permission. I can't leave the town unprotected. You see that, don't you?"

"You just finished telling me you got two new deputies. Oh what difference does it make anyway, you looked and looked and couldn't find Kilbane. You'll never find Leighton either; how can you find somebody dead and buried without the faintest idea where?"

"Let's have a cup of tea."

"I don't need tea!" she flared. "I've drunk gallons of it. It doesn't calm me down, doesn't relax me, doesn't do a damned thing. Besides, you have to leave as soon as possible. I know you'll never find him. I feel like I'm drowning, grasping at shadows on water!"

Fancy could only stand and listen; there appeared nothing left she could say that might ease her pain, nothing she was willing to accept. The only thing that would pull her up out of the morass of her despair would be his return.

She kissed her on the cheek, patted her hand consolingly and getting down, went back to the office. Elmer Stockton and the other deputy were out, but she found a visitor waiting for her. Mayor Dolfuss was in the rear talking to Alfred Gantner. Hearing their voices triggered an idea.

Alfred. He might come in handy. It may be unorthodox, even wild, and completely contrary to "the book," but what if she were to take him with her to Canadian? Unarmed, of course, and keeping an eye on him constantly. He knew Jake Webber and the others who had joined Kilbane's gang on sight. She wouldn't know any of them if she fell over them in the street. Every outlaw involved in the bank robbery had worn a bandanna over his face. She had thought she recognized Kilbane by his clothing; she was sure of it, as a matter of fact. But the operation had been so well planned, they had come out of the bank, each man holding a hostage as a shield and backing down the alley, not a single verbal command had been given. It had been carried out with military precision.

As to Alfred. If she did bring him along and he helped her it certainly wouldn't hurt him at his trial. Still, she had to be realistic; Dolfuss wouldn't hear of it. She pictured him shaking his head, his jowls quivering. Maybe she could talk him into it. It had to be worth a try; the whole mess was drawing closer and closer to desperate measures time.

She showed him Sheriff Whittlesey's telegram and opened the conversation with the less controversial subject of the two. It turned out to be what he himself had dropped by to discuss with her. His expression matched the worry in his words regarding Leighton's continued absence. He did not even mention Sturges. She got the feeling listening to him that he was as concerned about her being in charge as he was over Leighton. She told him about her plan to get temporary help from the nearest U.S. Marshal's office or from the Texas Rangers. He approved wholeheartedly.

"I might be able to get one or two rangers to take over right away. I know a Captain Casey Devereaux; he was a close friend of my father's in the early days. Last I heard he was still active. I could wire San Antonio."

"By all means do! The quickah the bettah. Get somebody up heah by train, at least to Higgins, befoah dahk. Elmah could go and fetch him. It's a grand idea!"

His worry had deserted his round, red face. His plump shoulders sagged as he relaxed. There could be no better time to bring up the subject of Alfred, she thought. The worst he could do would be to turn her down. She asked him politely, sweetly to hear her out. He did so, his face darkening by degrees. Finally, he shook his head.

"It's crazy, craziest thing I evah heard, takin' a cold-blooded killah out of his cell, puttin' him on a hohse and lettin' him ride off free as the breeze."

"He wouldn't be free. If you think about it, it wouldn't be any different than if I'd captured him and was bringing him in. I'd ride behind him, I wouldn't let him out of my sight for two seconds. Leighton and I brought him in originally, smoked him out of that ranch house on the Glazier Road."

"Leighton and you, not you by you'hself. I don't like it, Deputy."

"Sheriff."

"Eh? Oh, yes, beg you'h pahdon. Slip o' the tongue. Y'all think about it, it's not just risky as can be, it's illegal. Y'all are supposed to be holdin' all three of 'em for the judge. You'h responsibility."

She refused to give in. She insisted she had to bring Alfred along, that without him she didn't stand a chance of finding Kilbane and the gang. And if she didn't find them, she'd certainly never find Leighton and Sturges.

"Are you sayin' thea'h togetahah?"

"No, only that Leighton and Sturges left here chasing them. They could have caught up with them beyond the point where Elmer and I and the posse were turned back by the storm. Mayor, they could be dead and buried." He gasped. "We have to be practical. On the other hand, it's possible they're still tracking them. What I'm trying to say is if I can locate Kilbane, the chances are fair to good I'll find Leighton and Sturges." She tapped the telegram in his hands. "I'll have plenty of help."

"What makes you so sure this is the same bunch that held up the bank heah in town? Woman's intuition?"

"They took the railroad payroll in Canadian. Kilbane is not your run-of-the-mill high line rider. You saw yourself how he held up the Farmers and Merchants. It was like clockwork. Nothing like the fumbling and bumbling performance those three inside put on for us. He's shrewd, he's clever and he only goes after the ripest plums. He doesn't bother with stage coaches or saloons or citizens who look like they might be carrying ten dollars, like the Gantners. If there's such a thing as class in crime, Kilbane is it."

Again he shook his head. "I don't know. I don't want to be a stumblin' block. Judas priest, I want that boy back heah safe and sound as much as Maude does. Aftah what happened to poor Henry Cleghohn to lose Leighton on top of it."

He paused, unwilling to continue, abruptly overcome by dejection.

"Mayor, please, that boy out back is the only face card we hold. I'll assume full responsibility."

"I'm sorry, I can't let you do it. Let me finish, please. Y'all can get on down to Canadian, work with the sheriff down theah. What do y'all need with the boy anyway, y'all know what this Kilbane looks like. Y'all been sayin' all along you know him."

"I do, but—"

"Then what do you need with the boy?"

"We may get lucky and bump into a couple of the gang in town, in Glazier, any town in the area. They've got money, they're going to want to spend it. Where else can they spend it but in a town? Alfred could spot them."

"I suppose."

"Then you agree?"

"I can't, don't y'all undahstand?" He got up from his chair, his expression grim, obstinate. His mind was made up. She could talk until she collapsed from exhaustion, there was nothing she could say to change it.

She shrugged. "If you won't, you won't."

"I said I can't!" he snapped irritably.

"You can't. If you'll excuse me, I'll go back to the telegraph office and get a wire off to Captain Devereaux."

"Good ideah, I mean a grand ideah!"

* * *

As she expected, he was gone when she returned to the office. Elmer Stockton had come back with the other deputy, a man by the name of Win O'Connor. He had ridden with them the night of Henry Cleghorn's murder. He was possibly the homeliest man she had ever met. He looked as if he'd be perfectly at home hanging from the limb of a tree by one arm in the jungle. But he could handle a gun and showed no signs of milk in his spleen. They had just come from visiting Stanley. Mention of it warned her not to stop by Dr. Hume's office to look in on him before she left. Certain as the sun hung in the sky, the mayor had run as fast as his fat legs could carry him to the doctor's office to spill the beans. She told Elmer and Win that she was leaving town, showing them Whittlesey's telegram. She told them also to check with Western Union for the answer to her wire sent to Captain Devereaux. Adding that a response should arrive within the hour.

She said goodbye and left, but no sooner was she out the door then the devil in her woke up and snatched her attention. Turning around, she went back inside, straight through the office, taking down the keyring as she went through the inner door.

"Whatcha' doin', Fancy?" asked Elmer.

She unlocked Alfred's cell and motioned him out. He emerged wearing a quizzical look. O'Connor joined Elmer in the doorway.

"I'm taking Alfred here along with me. When we run into your friend Jake Webber and the others, you're going to identify them for me."

He shrank back, his face flooding with fear. "I dasn't do thet!"

"You'd better. It'll go easier for you in court if you do. If you refuse to, it'll go a lot harder. It could turn out the difference between going to prison and hanging."

"They cain't hang me! I ain' kilt nobody nohow! Never, crosst my heart, swear to God!"

"You want to take a chance on that in front of the judge? It's Judge Bartholomew. Elmer, isn't he known as the hanging judge?"

Elmer nodded. "Tougher than Roy Bean or Isaac Parker."

Alfred's hand went to his throat and he swallowed.

"Let's go," she said.

"Fancy," said Elmer, "can I speak to you just a second private?"

She had expected it before she unlocked the cell door. She locked Alfred in and returned to the outer office. She repeated the explanation she had given Alfred. Elmer looked increasingly skeptical as she went on, scratching his chin, furrowing his brow.

"I'm taking responsibility. I'll be in touch. You'll hear from me sometime this evening or at the latest early tomorrow. Believe me, I know exactly what I'm doing."

They shrugged and exchanged questioning looks. She released Alfred a second time and minutes later, having borrowed Stanley's roan for him, they set out for Canadian.

Eleven

Alfred rode three lengths ahead of Fancy. She had warned him in terms even he could understand regarding what was expected of him, what he could and could not do. He had a habit of swallowing, his prominent Adam's apple riding up and down his throat whenever fear struck his heart. But he swallowed harder and more painfully than she had ever seen him when she completed her instructions with the warning that if he tried to get away, whatever the circumstances, she would shoot to kill.

In her haste to leave, she had overlooked one thing which could be of value when she introduced herself to Sheriff Whittlesey, a note from Mayor Dolfuss. Her badge wasn't enough. If Whittlesey was anything like the majority of peace officers, he would shake hands, look her up and down, smirk, perhaps even laugh out loud when she told him she was acting sheriff.

Perhaps he wouldn't; maybe the urgency, even desperation implicit in his telegram would encourage him to welcome her without a barrage of questions. Bringing Alfred along could only help. Anyone could pin on a badge, but people impersonating the law weren't usually accompanied by prisoners. As they rode along, Alfred wanted to talk; she wanted to think and told him so.

Why was she doing this, going against Dolfuss's explicit orders, openly, brazenly defying him? The answer was easy; she didn't care in the least what he thought of her or what he would do or try to do when she came back. If he demanded her badge she'd be happy to give it to him. Nor did she care about Lipscomb in general. Leighton Haverstraw's welfare, along with Orrin Sturges's meant next to nothing to her. If she were to come upon either of them wounded, she would do her best to help them, as she would any human being, regardless of her personal feelings. But it was for Maude that she was sticking her neck out, openly inviting the axe.

Maude and herself. She couldn't in honesty overlook that. If there was one thing she had become convinced of over the past two hectic hours it was that if she got lucky and found Kilbane, she would find Haverstraw. And viceversa. It was all conjecture, to be sure, linking him, Sturges and Kilbane. On second thought, as much wishful thinking as conjecture. But there was still the assault on Stanley in the alley, the fact that he had been shot in the back. *He* certainly hadn't told Kilbane about the lookout; she hadn't; that left Haverstraw and Sturges. One of them must have warned him. There was of course the slender possibility that the one that had hadn't bothered to tell the other. But this her intuition rejected.

"They're with him, they've got to be."

"You say somethin'?"

"No."

"I could swear I heerd you."

"You're hearing things."

"If you say so."

She studied him from the back. Another child gone wrong. Correction, led wrong by his beloved family, poor creature. He had grown up force fed the philosophy that what others had you were free to take from them, just make sure you don't get caught. Excitement, profit and a chance to see the world of the West on the run. Just see that you keep your distance from the law and the hangman.

"How to get ahead in life."

"You say somethin'?"

"Alfred, you speak when you're spoken to, understand?"

"Yup." The was a resonant pause. Their horses' hooves thudded the road in rhythm. "On'y I did think I heerd you."

"Shut up!" she burst irritably, and instantly regretted it.

Why take her frustration out on him? She thought about Maude. Her friend. The one word said it all: trust, faith, dependability, warm and comfortable companionship, all and more. My friend Maude. And what was Maude's friend up to at the moment? Riding out to find Maude's husband dead or alive; either way, guilty of complicity in crime. Two already committed and others to come.

It was discouraging the way Kilbane affected her life without his even knowing he was. She had come to Lipscomb to find him and had, standing helplessly by and watching him rob the bank. Within her first half hour in town she had made a new friend whose husband was now involved with Kilbane. And here she was, riding out to find Leighton and the proof of their association. Proof that would have to be ironclad, to be sure. Which wouldn't change Maude's mind about him. It would change her mind about her friend, however. Maude was scrupulously honest, as straight as straight as fence wire, but no matter how overwhelming the evidence might be against her Leighton, she would reject it, close her ears and turn her back. To accept it would be tacit admission that her judgment was faulty, that she had carelessly permitted her heart to play her for a fool. And she'd made the biggest blunder of her young life. It was highly unlikely she would be grateful to her friend for bringing it to Lipscomb's attention. The tongues of the town would cherish it for years to come and Maude would never forgive her.

By the time they reached Canadian, a little more than ten miles to the south, Fancy had all but completely changed her mind about the entire affair. She was prepared to ride right through town without so much as a glance at the sheriff's office. Get out of Hemphill County, out of Texas, put it all behind her. But she could not. There was Alfred, there was her commitment to Henry Cleghorn that went with accepting the badge on her pocket. There was Kilbane. Tossing away this chance to catch up with him and settle things once and for all made no sense. There was Maude. If she had to be hurt, so be it. Better that than a marriage built on deceit to a man incapable of loving anybody but himself.

Was that true? Even if it were, what business was it of hers? Maude had chosen him. She hadn't asked for her advice at the time, she wasn't asking it now. Advice or interference in her life.

What a mess, the perfect no-win situation!

"Pull up, Alfred."

"You can call me A. J., evvybody does."

"Mmmmm."

Fancy looked about before entering the sheriff's office. Canadian appeared to be five times the size of Lipscomb. The Southern Kansas Railroad running through it was the chief stimulus to growth. Without a railroad Lipscomb would never grow, would probably shrink in population in the years to come.

A deputy was on duty. He looked little older than Alfred. His eyes were pale blue and as empty of intelligence as unstamped five-cent pieces. He was all knees and elbows, with a turkey neck, an upturned nose and thin, mobile lips.

"Can I help you?"

"I'm looking for Sheriff Whittlesey."

"He's out chasin' with the boys. I'm the only deputy in town." He polished his badge with his fist and grinned. "You got a badge, too." He frowned. "But you're a woman. You a deputy?"

"That's what it says."

"For real, honest?"

"Do you have any idea when the sheriff will be back?"

"Nope. Didn't say. Didn't know. He just comes in to eat and sleep. Been running all over north Texas looking for 'em. You're a woman, a woman deputy."

From the astonishment on his face she well might have had two heads, she thought.

"Where's the express office?"

His skinny arm rose, his finger pointing at the wall to his left. "Two doors down. It was robbed. Is he a deputy too?"

"He's a prisoner. Lock him up for me."

"What'd he do?"

"A little of everything." She got out Whittlesey's telegram, handing it to him. He stared at it blankly. "It's a telegram. Sheriff Whittlesey sent it to us in Lipscomb."

"I can't read."

She read it to him. He nodded.

"That's what they done, all right. A woman deputy."

"What's the Wells, Fargo agent's name?"

"Enoch Chambers. Most jumpiest man alive. Bundle o' nerves. These doings got him sick."

He continued to sit, tilting his chair back, his long, lank fingers intertwined across his dirty shirt. She was beginning to think it would take dynamite to get him to his feet. She eyed the key ring on the wall. She got it down and handed it to him.

"I have to go see Mr. Chambers. Lock him up and keep and eye on him. I'll be needing him shortly."

"Is he dangerous? What's his name? What's your name?"

"His name's Alfred."

Stupid brightened. "That's my name, Alfred Bolton Junior. Your last name Bolton too?"

"Gantner."

The deputy's face fell.

"*I'll* lock him up," said Fancy impatiently. She did so, restoring the keyring to its nail. Deputy Alfred Bolton, Jr. still had not stirred from his chair.

"I'll be back," she said.

"You're a woman, a woman deputy."

She left him in the throes of his continuing astonishment.

The Wells, Fargo office, constructed of fireproof red brick, with its familiar iron shutters painted green at the windows, occupied a corner. Inside, Fancy was greeted by sight of a neat, well-planned office dominated by a solid wall of strongboxes and furnished with expensive-looking mahogany desks and chairs. On the wall above Enoch Chambers's desk an ornate document was displayed, certifying his "agency appointment" and declaring that the company had the following powers, viz:

> "To receive and receipt for Money, Valuables and Merchandise to be forwarded, to receive Notes, Drafts, etc., for collection, and to receive money to procure Bills of Exchange, certificates of Deposit, and for the purchase of Goods. The said Agent is not

authorized to draw any Check or Bill of Exchange, to receive any Deposit of Money or Valuables; not to undertake any transaction in the Company's name that does not legitimately pertain to the Express and Forwarding business."

Mr. Chambers sat at his desk in his shirtsleeves, his jacket draped over the back of his chair. He was white: hair, complexion, false teeth, hands and most of his eyes when he focused them on her.

"Who are you, what do you want?"

She introduced herself and handed him Whittlesey's telegram. It seemed to calm him down when he read it, but only slightly. Deputy Bolton was right, the man was "wire-edged with the wobbly horrors," as her Uncle Justin would say. Not surprising; he was in the frying pan for the payroll. The company was ensured against the loss, but if the money was not recovered its premiums would reflect a dramatic rise when the next payment on the policy fell due. He motioned her to a chair.

"Mr. Chambers, where were you when the office was robbed?"

"Here at my desk. It was noontime. Can you imagine? Talk about brass. Six of them came barreling in waving guns, one pushing two customers into that corner there, another holding his gun to my chest, my head, my back. He kept changing." He demonstrated with his finger. "I thought I was a goner for sure. My heart beat so it felt like it was going to jump out of my chest!"

There was a tumbler half-filled with water on his desk. He got out a pill box and downed four small, bright red pills.

"Excuse me. I'm not a well man. I wasn't before they showed up. They were in and out of here in less then five minutes. Bolted the front door, drew the shades, forced me to open the strongbox with the payroll."

"Only the one box?"

"Right. Ninety thousand dollars cold cash. Actually, ninety-two thousand one hundred fifty. If I hadn't done it, if I'd tried to stall for time or whatever by you know, opening the wrong box, they would have shot me, Mrs. Chakirides and Mason Hillcraft in cold blood." He shivered. "It was the scariest thing I've ever been put through. I've been agent here eleven years; this is the first time we've been robbed in daylight. Twelve noon, can you imagine?" He paused and drank some water. And held forth a trembling hand. "Look at me, look what they've done to me!"

"Can you describe them?"

"They all had neckerchiefs over their faces."

"What about their eyes, hair, coloring. Short, tall, fat, skinny?"

"One of them was about six-eight. A giant. Light blond hair. I didn't see his eyes, didn't dare look. Big, broad." He spread his hands. He described his clothing.

He described Orrin Sturges.

"Six feet eight," she mused aloud. "How about six foot six?"

He scowled. "I didn't take the trouble to measure the scoundrel!"

"What about the others? Tell me everything you remember, please, it's very important."

"I've already been through all this with Clayton Whittlesey."

"Tell me."

He described the other outlaws with surprising detail for one under such great stress, with death at the front end of the barrel placed against various sites on his body. She recognized Moss Kilbane as one of them, but not Haverstraw. None of the six descriptions fit the mental portrait of him fixed in her mind as she listened.

This didn't necessarily mean that he wasn't riding with Kilbane. Sturges definitely was. Chambers had said there were six. The farmer who had given her water had told her he'd passed a man fitting her description of Kilbane on the road. Two other men had been with him at the time. Alfred Gantner had later told her that six members of his brother's gang, including Jake Webber, had joined Kilbane. Add Orrin Sturges and it made a total of ten.

Haverstraw, eleven.

She had counted nine at the Farmers and Merchants robbery. She and Chambers talked for over an hour. The sun was sitting on the rim of the distant hill spoked like a golden wagon wheel when she emerged from the office and returned to the sheriff's. She was in luck. Whittlesey had come back. He sat in the chair previously occupied by his deputy, covered with red dust, ill-tempered from exhaustion and frustration from his failure to find the outlaws, in no mood to even discuss the situation.

"I asked Lipscomb for men. Plural. What in hell's the matter with Haverstraw?"

She explained. He listened, biting his lower lip, sinking deeper and deeper into the doldrums.

"I've never worked with a female deputy."

"First one I've ever seen," announced Bolton, standing with his back to the wall.

"Shut up, Alfred, I'm talking."

"Yup."

"It's crazy. Doesn't make a lick o' sense. You ride with us you could get your head shot off."

"You could too, whether I ride with you or not. Sheriff, I wouldn't be here if I couldn't do the job. I'm here to help, do you want me or don't you? Make up your mind."

"Okay, okay, don't get huffy. If that ain't just like a woman. You just come as a surprise, that's all. When I sent that wire the last thing I expected. Oh hell, never mind." He sighed heavily, wearily, and threw his head back, clamping his eyes tightly shut in an effort to press the fatigue out of mind, she thought.

"I'm so tired I can't keep my eyes open. We're done for today. We'll be starting out again tomorrow bright and early. Oh Jesus Christ, what am I saying? What am I doing! I'm sorry, Miss, I can't do it. I can't use you. Nothing personal, I got nothing against women. Hell, I'm married twenty-nine years come December. It's just I can't take you on. I don't dare."

"Whatever you say." She got up from her chair. "I'll just take my prisoner and get out of your hair."

"I'm sorry, honest."

"Me, too. But from what I can see it wouldn't work even if you tried it. Not the way you feel."

"You don't understand."

"I evidently don't. Let's leave it at that, okay?"

He got Alfred out of his cell for her. "What did you bring him for?"

"He knows some of the people riding with Kilbane. He'd recognize them. Who knows, a couple might be drifting around here or Glazier. I need him."

"You mean you're fixing to go chasing on your own? I can't allow that, not in Hemphill county. It's my jurisdiction and what I say goes."

"Of course. Good luck, Sheriff, it's been a pleasure."

"You don't have to be sarcastic."

"I apologize. It hasn't been a pleasure."

"Wait a second. You say he knows what some of them look like? How about leaving him here in my custody?"

"I can't do that, I don't have the authority."

"Wait, wait, where you going now?"
"Back to Lipscomb."
"What's the grand rush?"
"Goodbye, Sheriff."

She marched Alfred out, taking pains to slam the door behind them.

Twelve

Fancy had no more intention of going back to Lipscomb than of robbing the Wells, Fargo office.

"Where to now?" asked Alfred.

"Glazier."

"What for?"

"Don't ask so many questions, Alfred, just keep cooperating. You're doing beautifully."

"I ain' done nothin' yet."

"You're keeping me company, aren't you?"

They rode side by side following the railroad tracks to the northeast. The uneven land was swathed with dark brown shadows, spreading as they lengthened. Canadian huddled behind them. A column of smoke broke the horizon ahead. A train was approaching, the engine's diamond stack defining itself against the purple sky. She could feel her horse tense slightly. She moved them off the road paralleling the tracks, continuing on through a fallow field studded with rocks. Closer and closer drew the train, then thundered by, its bell clanging, brakes squealing, slowing it as it neared Canadian.

"I like trains," said Alfred. "I wisht I was on a train. I'm hungry."

"So am I. We'll eat in Glazier."

"Then what?"

"Look around town."

Glazier was smaller than Lipscomb and deader, from all appearances. The only restaurant in town—displaying the designation on a large, crudely painted sign above the door—proved to be nothing more than a counter boasting nine stools. They ate beef stew in a silence imposed and sternly enforced by Fancy. The day's events had left her in no mood for conversation. She had all but talked herself dry with Enoch Chambers, and she had been too upset, too disgusted with Whittlesey to bother trying to persuade him to accept her help. But on the way to Glazier she made up her mind to return to Canadian and stay the night. Arising early the next morning, she planned to keep an eye on Whittlesey's door and when he and his men came out to go hunting she would follow. It would be better than striking out alone, looking for the needles in the hay. The sheriff had to be following some sort of prearranged pattern that enabled him to cover the four neighboring counties in the northeast corner of the Panhandle to avoid wasting time searching the same area twice. Of course there was no assurance that Kilbane was staying in one place between jobs. He could even be riding two miles behind him, stalking *him*, purely for amusement. Such a tactic would appeal to his twisted sense of humor.

She sighed to herself. It was all coming loose at the seams, falling apart. As far as she could see there were only two things that might possibly work in her favor. One was that Kilbane would pull a third job and hopefully she would be close enough to him at the time to hear about it and get after him while the trail was still hot. Such trails got very

The Odds Against Sundown 115

cold very soon, unfortunately. Witness the Wells, Fargo holdup. The second figurative arrow in her figurative quiver was the possibility that one or more of Alfred's former associates might come to town. Any town. The only thing wrong with that was that in the four counties, Lipscomb, Hemphill, Ochiltree and Roberts in that area there were five towns, rendering the odds five to one against her being in the right place at the right time. Being there at the right time would be a heavenly wrought miracle! In addition to which, what made her think Kilbane planned to restrict his activities to the four counties? He could go where he pleased, as far as he pleased. He could be sitting drinking in Dallas at that very moment.

She gave up halfway through her stew. It was watery, too salty, and the beef chunks more fat and gristle than meat. The coffee was lukewarm and tasted like someone had substituted alum for sugar. She imagined it sticking to the inside of her mouth. Alfred loved the stew, finishing a second bowl and taking two refills of coffee. He was starting his third cup when his eyes strayed to the grimy window and he stiffened.

"Anson."

"Who?"

"Anson Fayles. I'd know thet hair anyplace. Long as Buffalo Bill Cody's, on'y black 'stead o' white."

She flung money down on the counter. She grabbed him by the shoulder. "Let's go."

"I ain' finished my coffee. I ain' hardly started."

"I said move!" she burst, drawing every eye in the place and stilling every mouth.

Fayles and his companion were a block ahead of them and turning into a saloon by the time she got outside with Alfred.

"Who's that with him?"

"Cain't tell from the back. Could be his brother Ira Tom. Mebbe not. I didn' really see. But that there's Anson, all right. Can we go into there an' have us a drink or two?"

"No."

"Can I go back now an' finish my java?"

"No."

"You mean we got to stan' 'round waitin' fer them to come out?"

"Exactly."

"They could be in there two hours!"

"They could be in there four." She pointed across the street. "We'll get our horses and stand in that alley and watch the door."

No sooner had they reached the alley and taken up their vigil then the two men came out of the saloon, arms around each other's shoulders, laughing raucously. Music and babble followed them out. Fancy and Alfred followed them out of town. A second glimpse of Anson Fayle's companion of the evening was no help to the boy. He claimed he had never seen the man before. She had no reason to doubt it. At any rate, one was all she needed.

They rode for a little more than three miles toward the Oklahoma border. Fancy maintained a distance of better than half a mile between them. The last thing she needed was to be spotted and turned on. This was the first real break in the case. It had to pay off, and big. It was up to her to make it, she thought.

The road snaked around hillocks, hills and outcroppings. Again and again she and Alfred lost sight of them around a corner only to pick up their dust once more. Each time it happened she held her breath until they got around the corner. They rounded an unusually long turn. She strained her eyes, peering ahead and damned under her breath.

There was no sign of them. No dust, nothing. She slackened the pace.

"I cain't see nobody nohow," said Alfred, mystified.

"They've cut off the road. Either that or caught sight of us and are waiting up ahead to ambush us."

"Tha's bad."

"We'll play it safe. Follow me and keep close."

She heeled the Barb, reining sharply right, vaulting over the rain ditch into knee-high grass. Low hills loomed ahead, the land getting its back up in a dozen different places. There was still no sign of the two riders, no sound. She didn't like it; the abruptness of their disappearance was almost weird. It was as if the earth had opened and swallowed them. An eerie feelng pervaded her. Back came her father's words: You can't shoot what you can't see, but it can shoot you.

"It" did. A single shot split the silence, cracking through the warm, dry gathering gloom of the night. Alfred cried out, started up in his stirrups, stiffened and tumbled from his saddle, his neck snapping with a sickening crunching sound as his head struck the ground. She threw herself down and flattened in the grass. Shots from a rifle chunked into the ground all around her. She eyed the 10-gauge in its scabbard, Lady standing motionless less than six feet away. Too far to try for. She got out her sixgun and held it in readiness, but instinct stopped her as she was preparing to lift her head for a look. Lift up and show them the target they wanted, she thought. She stayed where she was, still as a stone, her cheek pressed hard against the ground. Presently, the shooting let up, then ceased altogether. You can't hit what you can't see. She strained her ears. A light breeze arose, whispering through the grass, caressing, bending it. Moments later the muffled sound of hoofbeats reached her hearing.

By the time she got back to her horse and the 10-gauge the two men had vanished, sight and sound. She went to Alfred, kneeling beside him. He lay on his back, his head at an awkward, unnatural angle, an expression of panic on his face, his innocent eyes wide, his hair mussed and holding wisps of grass. A hole the size of a dime centered his heart. There was no blood, only the little red hole.

"Alfred, Alfred."

She stroked his hair, pushing it from his forehead. She closed his eyes. She brought Stanley's horse and slung the body belly down over the saddle. She mounted up and set out for Canadian, thinking as she started down the road leading the horse and its burden, planning the hour to come. Once arrived in town she would turn the body over to the local mortician, then look for a place for the night. She would stick to her original idea, get a night's sleep, get up early and follow Whittlesey and his men in their search.

It would be a discouragingly poor substitute for following Anson Fayles straight back to Kilbane and the others, where he and his companion had to be heading, but that break had come and was now gone, never to be retrieved.

Thirteen

Hostetter Brothers Funeral Parlor showed a solitary feeble light in the preparation room in the rear through the inner door as Fancy rode up. She tried the front door; it was locked. The window drapes were drawn. She rattled the door with a vigorous knock, paused, and knocked again, bringing a small man with a large head crowned with an ill-fitting transformation, youthful brown hair in startling contrast to his snow-white eyebrows and the salt and pepper stubble shadowing his jaw.

"Clothed for the day," he lisped, two droplets of spittle arcing forth from his mouth.

She indicated Alfred's body draped over Stanley's saddle.

"Oh," said the man, "ith' an emergenthy, why didn't you thay tho?"

He introduced himself as Leon Hostetter and helped her bring the body inside. Together, they laid it on a table in one corner. In the center of the room under a sheet lay another corpse, the face covered, only the feet showing. Fancy was suddenly surrounded by shelves and cabinets displaying scalpels, augers, scissors and forceps, needles, clamps, tubes, pumps, basins, and bowls. Tins and bottles, fluids, pastes, sprays, oils, powders and creams, paints, waxes and cosmetics. And over all the products and paraphernalia of the trade hung the powerful aroma of alcohol and formaldehyde mixed. Hostetter touched the wound with the tip of his finger.

"Bullthéye."

He undid Alfred's shirt, revealing his bare, hairless chest. There followed a flurry of questions. Fancy told him what had happened. As she did so he stared at her badge, his eyes questioning; that is, he appeared to be staring at her badge. But it was possible that her breast supporting her tin was what was claiming his attention.

"Thath' all very interethting, Deputy, but in catheth of thith nature ith' cuthtomary to make an official report and thend a copy to Authtin. Thath' the law."

"I understand."

"Very well. Thereth' a ten dollar fee, pluth burial expentheth. Who geth the bill?"

She got out her money. "I'll pay for everything now, if you don't mind."

"I don't mind in the leatht."

The odors, the surroundings, the implements, the workings of matter over mind were beginning to nauseate her. Pay him and get out of here, she thought, and did so, pausing briefly before leaving to take one last look at Alfred. Her heart sank as she pushed his hair off his forehead.

Outside it was rapidly getting dark. Across the street stood the Canadian Hotel, a ramshackle edifice that looked as if a stiff north wind would level it. She started for it. Music from the saloon Anson Fayles and his friend had stepped into could be faintly heard:

"It's step to your weev'ly wheat,
It's step to your barley,
It's step to your weev'ly wheat
To bake a cake for Charley."

To bake a cake for Alfred, she thought. What a waste. Bring a child into the world, suckle and nurture and raise him. And bend, twist him, his character, his view of right and wrong. Set his feet in the wrong direction. Commit his life to greed, violence and danger. Guarantee him a premature and ignominious death. His older brother Mace, who he spoke so fondly of, idolized, should have been strangled in the cradle!

A stray dog chased another down the street, barking raucously. A couple came reeling out of the saloon arms wrapped tightly around each other. A window in a room on the second floor of the hotel was lifted open and a woman settled her bulk on the sill, evidently to catch a breath of fresh air. Shops and stores stood dark and forlorn looking, buttoned for the night and Canadian prepared to retire.

She crossed the street and was about to ascend the steps to the lobby when a voice called to her out of the alley to her right, the same alley she and Alfred had watched the saloon from earlier. A man emerged, walking unsteadily, threatening to drop with every step. He was disheveled and exhausted looking.

Leighton Haverstraw.

Fancy gasped and gaped. "You."

He smiled weakly, his hand rising to the side of the building seeking support. She went quickly to him.

"What on earth? What's happened? Where have you been? Maude's been out of her mind with worry!"

"I know, I know, it's a long story." He set his back against the side wall and slid slowly down to a sitting position, his head lolling to one side. "I'm so beat I can't even hold my head up. I must have walked twenty miles." He brightened slightly. "But I got away. I still don't believe it but I did."

"It's been a week, more like a year to her. You might have wired her."

"That's just it, I couldn't."

"You'll have to wait till tomorrow morning. Western Union's locked up tight."

"I know, I know." His tone was becoming frayed with impatience. "Do you want to hear about it or don't you?"

"Of course, but first, are you all right? Are you wounded?"

"No, just famished and worn down to a nub. A steak and a good night's sleep and I'll be all right."

He and Sturges had followed Kilbane and the gang to the Oklahoma border and over it to Shattuck, south of Wolf Creek. Then, for some reason, the outlaws had circled and recrossed the border, coming back into Texas. In the dead of night sheriff and deputy had sneaked up on their camp, but before either could get a shot off.

"Sturges turned on me, Fancy. There I stood looking into the barrel of his .45. I couldn't believe my eyes. That son of a bitch was the worst mistake I've ever made! Oh lady, butter wouldn't melt in his mouth the way he sold himself to me."

"What happened next?"

"The back breaker. Come to find out he wasn't even in cahoots with them. It was an impulse. On the spur of the moment he decided to try to get in using me. He marched me to their fire, told your friend Kilbane he wanted to join them and I was proof of his 'good faith'. It worked; Kilbane took him on." He fumbled in his pocket and showed a star. "Sturgis gave me back his badge. That was a big laugh all around." He paused and looked across the street. "Where's your horse?"

"Over there in front of the funeral parlor. Right beside Stanley Firestone's roan."

"Stanley. If he'd done his job and warned us none of this would have happened. When we get back, Mr. Firestone is going to have a lot of explaining to do!"

"He couldn't warn anybody. He was shot in the back."

His jaw dropped. "Before they showed up?"

"Probably just as."

"Is he dead?"

"He came close. He's on the mend now."

"My God, I didn't know." He shook his head in disbelief. "You wouldn't by chance have Stanley's gun? No, of course not."

She told him about Alfred, her reason for bringing him with her. It didn't seem all that important as she listened to herself. Besides, she was more interested in what he had to say.

"How did you get away from them?"

"Mostly luck. Do you remember the ranch house on the Glazier road where we had that set-to with the two kids?"

"Kilbane is there?"

"No, no, they're over the county line in Roberts. Holed up in a shack the kids' older brother and his bunch were using before they cleared out. One big room filled with cots and groceries and loot. It's well hidden and easy to defend. They don't even bother posting a guard. The ranch house was where we stopped on the way there, to pick up supplies and what not. I got away after we reached the shack and settled in. Kilbane had one of them tie me up every night. His name is Webber. He rode with the two kids' older brother. Six of them joined Kilbane."

"I know."

The night he escaped, Webber had been drinking. Everybody was, except Kilbane. Webber got so drunk he neglected to tie him properly. While they slept he easily freed himself, climbed through an open window and ran.

"Why didn't you take a horse?"

"I was afraid the sound would wake somebody up. If it did I wouldn't have gotten half a mile. Before I climbed through the window I tried to take Webber's gun, but when I lay my hand on the grip he stirred. I panicked. I just wanted out of there."

His biggest fear was that somebody would wake up shortly, wake the others and chase him. If that happened he figured they would figure he'd head straight for Lipscomb. To cross them up he headed for Canadian. By the time he was halfway there he was so exhausted he found a gully, collapsed in it and slept away most of the day.

"Nerves," she said.

"And not enough sleep the nights before. Listen, I know Clayton Whittlesey. He was a close friend of Henry's."

"We've met. I offered to help in the search. He turned me down."

"Sounds like Clayton, all right. Fancy, there's a lot more, and I know you've got a lot to tell me, but it can wait. If I don't get something in my stomach I'll pass out."

She helped him to his feet. They crossed the street to what looked to be the only restaurant in town still showing lights. It was mobbed with locals and drovers. He ordered a steak. When it arrived he wolfed it down ravenously, choking more than once. When he was finished she took him back to the hotel and got him a room next door to her own. Then she went back down to stable the two horses for the night.

She came back to the hotel twenty minutes later and knocked on his door. He was asleep but woke up. He lay fully clothed on top of the bed. She sat at the foot, keeping a discreet distance between them. As they talked—she filling him in on what had transpired since he and Sturges left Lipscomb, he elaborating on what had happened to him—she began to perceive that he had changed. A different, almost completely new Leighton Haverstraw.

"Fancy, I realize I've given you a hard time since Henry was murdered. Even before I wasn't exactly warm and friendly."

"Not exactly."

"Let's be honest, I've been a nasty son of a bitch. To say I'm sorry now seems much too little too late. But I am, I mean it sincerely. From now on I'll do everything I can to make amends. All I ask is the chance to prove myself. I want to be your friend. It was my fault we never got along."

"It takes two."

"No, I'm to blame. When we get this mess straightened out and things are back to normal I'm going to make it up to you."

"You don't owe me anything, Leighton."

"Don't be so generous. I owe you everything, starting with my life in that shootout in the hills. I guess deep down I'm a bit of a bastard. I couldn't wait to turn on you the next day. Talk about two-faced . . ." He half-laughed. "I'm surprised you didn't come after me with your 10-gauge."

He was being genuinely contrite, he at least seemed sincere, looking into her eyes as he spoke, his voice modulated, his manner determined. She had never liked him from the first. Even in the minute of introductions before he began mauling her in the hotel room. Whatever he said now in the way of apology couldn't expunge that from memory. Nevertheless, it would be unfair of her not to at least meet him halfway. That had been Maude's idea all along, the magic means of resolving their differences.

The further he stretched his apology, the more regret he voiced for his behavior, the sorrier she felt for him. That was her trouble, she mused, she felt sorry for everybody: Wayland, Alfred, Maude, everybody but Kilbane.

He was tired, his voice betrayed it, but he had to talk, had to purge himself of his self-consciousness over their relationship. Three times he came back to their first meeting and apologized profusely for his actions. She let him talk himself out, then she changed the subject.

"What about tomorrow? I was planning to go out alone to look for them."

"We'll go together. All I need is a gun. If you could let me have a few more dollars . . . Webber cleaned me out and split it with that bastard Sturges. I had to stand there and watch them."

"We really should hook up with Whittlesey. Only as I say, he's already made it clear he doesn't want me around."

He thought about this for a moment. "Then to hell with him. He doesn't have the foggiest idea where to find them. He could beat the bushes for another month. Let's just go and take them ourselves."

"Two against ten?"

"We'll sneak up on them, just the way we did the two kids at the ranch house, one of us front, the other back. Get the drop on them. Take away their weapons and they'll be helpless. Ten, twenty, thirty, without guns they can't do a damned thing. We can surprise them easy; I've got to be the last person in the world they'd expect to show up."

"I don't know about that. My guess is they've already cleared out of there. If I were Kilbane I'd have to think that having gotten away you'd collect the biggest posse in history and head straight back. They're gone by now."

"Maybe."

"No maybes."

"We should go back and make sure. If they *have* left, ten men will leave a trail that should be easy to follow. There's only the one road in and out of there. I got away through the hills. We could follow the road and see where they cut off it. If we don't pick up their trail within say five miles, we'll just go back and go through the hills in the opposite direction."

There were many more directions than the two, but she let it pass.

"I want Kilbane and Sturges," he said, breaking into her thoughts. "The rest don't interest me. They can run to Mexico for all I care."

"You can have Sturges, I want Kilbane."

"Wait a minute."

"I'm not going to argue about it. I've been after him a long time. Even caught him. More than once. I've 'earned' him, Leighton."

"You sound like you plan to kill him on sight."

"Not unless he or somebody else forces me to. No, I'll bring him in, lock him up and see him tried for murder on twenty counts. Whatever the score comes to. You can bet it's impressive. God in heaven, if he were to be tried for every crime he's committed, to balance the ledger they'd have to hang him fifty times!"

"That bad?"

"Worse. The worst. He's mine."

He shrugged. "I won't get in your way. Not the way you handle a gun. But after what he did to me, Sturges is all mine. If I get that double-crossing son of a bitch in my sights and he so much as breathes, I'll put six shots in his face. I swear to God I will!"

His selection of a target reminded her of Alfred and Wayland at the ranch house, and how he had unhesitatingly shot the boy in the back. Wayland had been out of her line of sight around the corner of the house and it wasn't until after the bullet hit him that she reached the corner and saw. She recalled the hollowness of her gasp and the sudden surge of fury with Leighton. In her mind she saw his face again, his expression grim, but his eyes sparkling in triumph. Or was it glee? She remembered thinking at the time that he had enjoyed doing it. Now this changed man, this Leighton Haverstraw number two, no relation to number one he would have her believe, was stretched out opposite her offering to help catch Kilbane. Or rather asking her to help him.

Deep down she did not want him to change so radically, all but completely. Not that she had any fondness for his original. Far from it! Only that she was finding it difficult to accept him as he was presenting himself. It was as if his old personality had deserted his body to make room for this new, entirely different one. It was admirable, forthright of him, she was impressed. Only it strained believability.

He was too good to be true. She would keep an eye on him and keep intact a small reserve of suspicion at the back of her mind. Talk, after all, was cheaper than Texas dust. How he behaved in the hours to come would be the determining factor.

He read her thoughts. He stared at her fixedly. "You think I'm selling you a bill of goods, don't you? You still don't trust me."

"I didn't say . . ."

His hand came up. "You have every right, every precedent not to. Here I've been talking practically nonstop, apologizing, alibiing, explaining, everything but heap hot ashes on my head. I'm done now. Tomorrow I'll start proving myself. All I ask is that you reserve judgment until we've wound this up."

She nodded. "About Whittlesey, maybe we'd be making

a mistake not to ring him in. You might be able to change his mind about me."

"I might not. He's an old man, Fancy, old school. A woman's place, all that stuff. His attitude is burnt into his brain, like never trust an Indian. Actually, there's another reason to stay clear of him. To be honest, I'd like nothing better than to get him into the position where he owes me one. If we mop this up ourselves we'll be collaring the same bunch that robbed Wells, Fargo here in his town, right?" He chuckled. "That's one feather he'll never forgive me for stealing before he can stick it in his cap. You can't imagine what that would mean to me."

"You sound like two little boys squabbling over marbles."

"There's little boy in every man."

"Some more of it than others."

He ducked his head behind his hand, pretending sheepishness. She laughed.

Fourteen

Before Breakfast the next morning Haverstraw went to Western Union to get off a telegram to Maude.

"She should get it within the hour," he said, returning to Fancy, waiting for him on the hotel verandah.

She had bought a sixgun for him and cartridges. They caught a quick bite and went straight to the sheriff's office. Whittlesey and four deputies were preparing to leave on their daily search. He seemed surprised at the sight of Haverstraw.

"Where in tophet have you been? We've been looking as much for you as those owlhoots."

He explained briefly. Three of the deputies stood staring at him as he talked, the fourth stared at Fancy. She turned away from him, but was unable to lose his eyes.

"We're going with you, Clayton," said Haverstraw in conclusion.

The sheriff's eyes also wandered to Fancy. She noted the disapproval in them.

"You're more'n welcome to come, but . . ."

"Deputy Hatch comes too. I'll vouch for her. She may not have told you, but she saved my life last week."

"I don't know, Leighton."

"I do! Let's quit the jawing and head on out. I know where they're holed up. Do you want them or don't you?"

"That's a dumb question."

"Then she comes along. Let's go."

Putting the rising sun at their backs, they headed west, Fancy and the two sheriffs riding abreast. Whittlesey fired question after question at Haverstraw concerning his captivity and escape. Then:

"You got any ideas where they might hit next?"

"That shouldn't be hard to figure, if they're still around. They've already hit Lipscomb and Canadian."

"And Glazier yesterday."

"Is that right?" asked Fancy.

"Cleaned out the bank just before closing time."

Haverstraw reacted wordlessly. "That leaves Higgins, Ochiltree and Miami in the four counties. There's nothing worth the taking in Ochiltree. So next is either Higgins or Miami."

"Mangy mongrels!" burst Whittlesey. "What brass! They're going through this neck o' the woods like a reaper through a wheat field. Turn us upside down then move on."

"There's a lot of grain money here and they know it. And knowing Kilbane he won't leave a dollar behind."

"He *is* very thorough," conceded Fancy.

They crossed the Roberts County line into hilly country. Miami lay to the south about six miles, strung along a shelf between a steep hill and Red Deer Creek.

"Every street in town runs uphill," asserted Whittlesey. He chuckled. "Unless o' course you're heading the other way. Kilbane will probably be looking to hit there before he does Higgins. There's the bank and the only post office in the county there. Two for the price o' one." Again he laughed.

Presently, Haverstraw slackened his pace. The others followed suit. He pulled up and pointed ahead.

"The hideout is around that bend behind the hills to the left. How do you want to go in, Clayton?"

"Surround the place. How the hell else? Excuse me, ma'am. Go barreling in blazing away. Catch 'em with their boots off!"

"Shouldn't one of us go first and take a look?" asked Fancy. "They may not even be there."

Haverstraw agreed.

"Go take a look," said Whittlesey to him.

He spurred the roan and galloped away, cutting off the road and around a hill out of sight. They waited. A hawk floated high overhead. Waiting for the show to start, she thought, eying it. Whittlesey glanced at her, but did not speak. He didn't have to; she knew what was running through his mind. The look of disapproval still lingered in his eyes. You can't teach an old dog, she mused. Haverstraw reappeared waving them forward.

"They've cleared out."

"Son of a . . ." Whittlesey caught himself. "Sorry, ma'am."

She could have laughed in his face. It was the second time he had excused his language. The day before it was hell and damn and Jesus Christ. Evidently, he felt that if he couldn't accept her as a deputy, he had an obligation to as a woman and as a consequence had to curb his tongue. He went on.

"They sure didn't come this way. They must have cut through the hills in the back. Any ideas, Leighton?"

Fancy's eyes were on him. He felt them, looked straight at her and looked away.

"Miami?"

Whittlesey brightened. "Bet your boots and saddle!"

He raised his reins and was preparing to spur his horse when Haverstraw stopped him short, gesturing.

"Let's kick this around a little before we go rushing off. They could be heading for Miami . . ."

"Or Higgins."

"That's right. I see it as a toss-up. Why don't Deputy Hatch here and I head for Lipscomb, pick up whoever's taken my place there and some men and head for Higgins, while you fellows go on to Miami?"

"Fine with me."

Off rode the five of them without another word. He followed them with his eyes, his smile strange, crooked.

"The ranch house," she said flatly.

"Does it make sense? What do you think?"

"It's a possibility. Still, they did stop there with you on the way to this place. Wouldn't Kilbane assume you'd think that's where they've gone?"

"He no doubt does, but like coming here double checking, I'd hate to pass it up. We have to head pretty much in that direction anyway to get to the train tracks and follow them. Glazier's on our way. The house is only a mile or so out of the way. What do you think?"

It was the second time he had put that question to her within a minute's time. He did appear to be practicing today what he had preached the previous night. No more sarcasm, belittling; now courtesy, respect. They swung about and headed east, returning to within sight of Canadian and turning left for Glazier about seven miles away.

They reached the Glazier–Lipscomb road and started up it. Sooner then she expected they spied the house, low lying, lonely looking and shabby under the beautiful cloudless azure sky. Weeds were overrunning the front yard.

Fence rails had come loose and dropped, neglect slowly taking possession of the place. No horses could be seen outside as they approached, but galloping past the house at a good clip and veering off the road to circle the barn, Fancy felt instinctively that there were horses inside. Haverstraw seemed to feel no such instinct for when they reached the far side, he pulled up and checked at once, pressing his ear against a crack.

"They're in there. Sounds like a herd. There shouldn't be any. How do we handle this, Fancy?"

"Didn't you say the same as before?"

He grunted. "I've got a better idea. Let's keep going until we get to Lipscomb. I can stop off and see Maudie. We can collect a posse . . ."

"I don't know, Leighton, by the time we get back here they could be gone. We'd be no better off than Whittlesey, running all over the landscape."

He laughed mirthlessly. "You really do want Kilbane, don't you? I mean like a starving dog wants a bone."

"That's a pretty crude comparison, but I can't say you're wrong. And don't forget, we made a deal, he belongs to me."

"He's yours, Sturges is mine." He paused, studying her with his head canted to one side. "What you really want is to shoot him, don't you. It would be easier, cleaner than a courtroom. You may have to; give him half a chance and he'll sure try to kill you."

"We'll do this the same way, as you suggested. It's ancient, but it works."

"Let's hope."

They dismounted and led the horses behind the barn. They immediately began grazing on the long, sere grass. She started back down the side. He called to her.

"Fancy?"

"What?"

"Be careful."

She murmured response. She did not look back.

"Hey," he called.

This time she turned. And looked into the muzzle of his gun. Wreathing his face was the broadest grin she had ever seen there.

Fifteen

"What a delightful surprise!" burst Kilbane at sight of Fancy. He bowed, sweeping her into the room as if greeting nobility.

Haverstraw stood behind her. He shoved his gun into his belt. The others, among them Orrin Sturges, stood about grinning like apes.

"How in the world did you manage it, Leighton?"

"Didn't I tell you I would? Credit patience as much as intelligence."

"Amazing."

"Excellent, very thorough planning, even better execution."

"You missed your calling, you should have been an actor." Kilbane chuckled. Fancy glanced about. "Look at the lady, gentleman; look at her face, she's livid."

Haverstraw nodded. "With herself as much as me."

She was; she had never been so utterly, completely deceived in her life. One by one her firmly entrenched doubts had washed away, until the glass of opinion through which she viewed him was spotless, polished and gleaming.

137

By the time they had reached the Glazier–Lipscomb road and turned up it, so intent was she on getting to the ranch house to find out whether luck was with them or not, the last of her suspicions of Haverstraw had deserted her. Every step of the way from the alley alongside the hotel to this room had been calculated to win her over and at the same time follow a pre-set plan to bring her face to face with Kilbane with her defenses down. Haverstraw's smile was one of triumph; he wore it well, she thought; he should, he had earned it. He nodded to her, as if he had read her thoughts and was agreeing with her assessment of him. He cleared his throat meaningfully.

Kilbane looked from Fancy to him. "Oh, forgive me, Leighton. Here I'm so excited, so overwhelmed with your success I'm completely forgetting our arrangement. How much was it again?"

"Five hundred."

Kilbane counted out five $100 bills. "There we are, and thank you very much. I like a clean job well done. This is what you might call a bloodless coup, eh? So, Fancy, we meet again. Truly amazing. I was perfectly willing to give you the chance when you volunteered, Leighton, but in all honesty, never dreamed she'd buy your story."

"I didn't buy, I sold; there's a difference."

"Whatever you say, my friend. You're a clever man. And you, Fancy, are getting careless and gullible. You've never been either in our previous dealings. Speaking of which, when was the last time we saw each other?"

"Eureka."

"California, right. I was standing at the ship's rail and she shot at me from a roof top." He waggled a reproving finger. "You wounded me, although not badly." His hand went to his shoulder. "Still, I do know when wet weather is on the way. What was that, about two years ago?"

She said nothing. She stood looking from grin to grin. She had already recognized Jake Webber and long-haired Anson Fayles.

"Look at the lady, boys, she's no longer paying attention. Too busy thinking, planning her getaway."

"If she does get away Leighton'll go after her and fetch her back," blurted Sturges. "For five hundred more. Har har har."

"Nobody's asking you!" snapped Haverstraw.

"Easy, Leighton," interposed Kilbane. "Fancy, my dear, do take off your gloves. Make yourself comfortable."

"I'll keep them on, thank you."

He shrugged. "As you wish." He rubbed his hands together. "Well now, much as I'd like to, I'm afraid I don't have the time to stick around and continue resurrecting old times. We have work. You're welcome to come along if you like, or would you rather stay here and relax?"

She walked away from him. She set her hat on the table, sitting down hard in the only overstuffed chair in the room.

"Where to this time?" she asked. "All that's left are Higgins and Miami."

"Not Miami," said Haverstraw.

Kilbane turned toward him. "Why not?"

He told them about Whittlesey and his deputies.

"That was the one time in the whole performance I had my heart in my throat. I thought to myself, what if he insists we stick together, we go with him to Miami? How the devil will we get away so we can get back here?"

"How many men does he have?"

"Four, but he'll pick up at least ten more in town."

"Then Higgins it is. When we're done there we'll give him an hour or so to hear about it over the wire. He's been running around like an hysterical chicken. He'll head straight for Higgins. Meanwhile, we'll be out of the way and waiting someplace to the north of Miami. We'll give him time. . . . You all get the picture, I'm sure." One did not. Kilbane's dark eyes were on him. "Mr. Webber, am I confusing you?"

Jack Webber appeared to be in the grip of a painful hangover, his red and watery eyes pinched at the corners and suffused with suffering.

"Iffn' we don' hit the bank in Higgins."

Kilbane held his patience admirably, assuming a patronizing tone. "We're going to, I just told you. And before nightfall we'll visit Miami. Two in one day. And tonight we'll be leaving. All of you plan on riding all night."

A chorus of groans greeted this announcement.

"Where?" asked Haverstraw.

"West. As far as we can get in the next forty-eight hours. Leighton, I'd appreciate it if you tie her up. Necessary precaution. You see, Fancy, he rides, but he doesn't work with us. Not yet. He hasn't been involved in any of our ventures in the area. He has qualms about digging in his own backyard, so to speak. Isn't that so, Leighton?"

"It would be embarrassing if I happened across somebody I knew."

"I'm sure," said Fancy. "You're such a sensitive soul, you embarrass so easily."

"I do. You should get to know me better, you'd see."

"I know you as well as I want to, thank you."

Kilbane laughed. "Tie her carefully, Leighton. She's a tricky one."

Haverstraw set about his task. The others prepared to leave. He tied her wrists behind her back and her ankles securely, but without cutting off the circulation. Kilbane and his men filed out, talking in low tones, laughing, some casting covetous glances at her and leering. Moments later the house trembled slightly as they pounded off. Haverstraw stood at a front window watching.

"You never sent any telegram to Maude, did you?" He turned to her. "What a heartless, sadistic pig you are! You enjoy hurting her."

"Not a bit. I don't like that part of it, I definitely don't enjoy it. It's what you might call a necessary evil. What you must understand is, what's most important is the future. I ask myself over and over, where are you going to be five years from now? What doing? How well off will you be? A man's got to think of his future. I don't want to be stuck in Lipscomb the rest of my days. I want to get out in the world. I want money in my pocket. I want to do something with my life. The last thing I want is to sit in Henry's chair and grow old. There's no need to worry about Maudie; she'll get over me. Underneath all that sweetness and light she's tough, resilient. Oh yes, I left her; that's not exactly a capital crime. I changed my mind, that's all. I'm entitled. I'm certainly not leaving her penniless and starving. Her family's one of the wealthiest in north Texas.

"I must say I did think seriously about staying in Lipscomb; walking away from all that money—and she'll get every cent when the old folks pass on—wasn't easy. But of course it'll be ages before she gets her hands on it. Unfortunately I can't wait that long."

"Who are you trying to convince, me or yourself?"

"I don't have to convince 'me' of anything; my decision's made."

"And you're proud of it."

"Pride has nothing to do with it; it's strictly a question of priorities. I'm a very practical sort. A bird in the hand."

"One thing I can be thankful for, that's knowing that eventually you'll end up getting your head blown off."

"Possibly, but you won't be around to see it. And Maudie'll never know. By now I'm sure she's convinced

I'm already dead. I don't see anything happening to change her mind about that, do you?"

"You fascinate me. How do you live with yourself? How can you look in the mirror? Did you ever in your life have any semblance of a conscience?"

"You're wrong, dead wrong. Completely. For one thing I feel very sorry about Maudie. Honestly. Only a man has to do what's right, even if it means hurting somebody a little bit."

"You're incredible."

"Not really. Moss offered me a deal, me and Orrin, it made sense, we accepted it."

"Which of you shot Stanley? Why am I asking, you'll say Orrin, of course."

"He did. You don't think I shoot close friends, do you? I hope and pray he recovers completely, good old Stanley."

"I'll bet you can't sleep nights thinking about him, and Maude, all the people in Lipscomb who trusted you, believed in you. What did you do with the rifle they gave you for 'service to the community'?"

"It's still over the mantel in our dream house. Didn't you see it there? It's a beauty."

"You're the beauty."

"You flatter me. Thank you. But as I keep telling you, a man has to do what he thinks is right."

She half laughed. "You keep coming back to that word 'man.'"

"You don't think I'm a man?"

Her heart moved in her chest. It was the wrong tack to take, moving what was essentially a meaningless conversation, a means for letting out some of her frustration, in a new and serious direction. He was staring at her, his eyes glowing. It was a look she had seen too many times before, one that started fear in her. He licked his lips.

"You know something, Fancy, you're even more beautiful here and now than you were in that hotel room the time I came up to introduce myself. You were some surprise. I had no idea you'd look so." He came closer, crouching in front of her, his hands on her knees, his eyes searching hers. "Beautiful, sensuous, desirable. You have no idea how sensuous you are, what you do to the man in a man, what you're doing right now to me. I look at Maude, dear Maudie: vivacious, sweet, cute as a button, but a little girl. And always will be. You're a woman." Again he licked his lips and took a deep breath, letting it out slowly between clenched teeth. The lust glow in his eyes was deepening, becoming more intense.

"You musn't be afraid."

"What makes you think I am?"

"Your face. You look like a cornered doe. There's something fastastically exciting about a frightened woman, frightened, helpless, vulnerable, the way you breathe, your breasts, the way they move up and down. They're extraordinary. You are . . ."

"And you're a pig, disgusting, loathsome, the saddest excuse for a man I've ever met. I feel sorry for you."

"Do you really? Or is it that you're attracted to me, only you can't stand the thought of being. Love and hate butting up against each other. It's not uncommon."

She managed a disdainful laugh, but it came out thin, reedy, not at all convincing. His right hand came forward. He rose and began unbuttoning her blouse. She could see his member erecting, bulging at his crotch. He slipped his hand inside, cupping her breast, rubbing it slowly. She tried to pull free, but he gripped her shoulder with his other hand, his thumb pressing hard just under the bone, hurting.

"Stop it!"

"Shout. Scream your lungs out. Go on . . ."

"Bastard!"

"Bastard, pig, that's me. What magnificent breasts, so full, so warm . . ."

"I swear I'll kill you!"

"Of course. I can almost feel the daggers coming out of your eyes. Be honest, give in, admit I excite you. Why shouldn't you be aroused, you're only human." Kneeling, he untied her ankles. "What am I, but 'only human.' Life is strange, isn't it? If it had been different for both of us we might have gotten together years ago. Fallen in love, gotten married." His expression sobered. His voice became cold. His words seemed to be issuing forth from a robot. "I want you and I'm going to have you. Willingly or unwillingly. How, makes no difference. Of course if you do put up a fight it'll make it more exciting. Get up."

"This is going to be the sorriest day of your life."

"Mmmmm."

He pushed her ahead into the bedroom. The bed had been slept in, the covers rumpled. On the night table was a tintype in a brass frame on a stand showing a middle-aged couple arm in arm and smiling. They were old and dead now, she thought fleetingly, the owners of the house no doubt buried somewhere on the property. He was untying her wrists. Her blouse was completely unbuttoned, revealing the deep cleavage between her massive breasts.

"I'm going to leave you so you can undress in privacy. Everything off. I'll be right outside, so don't get any foolish ideas like climbing out the window. I'll be listening, I'll hear every sound. If you do something foolish I'll have to punish you. I wouldn't want to hurt you, so don't make me." He stepped back. It was what she had been waiting for. Room for leverage. She turned to face him. He smirked and the tip of his tongue touched his upper lip at the center. His breathing became husky as his lust grew. He reached for

The Odds Against Sundown 145

her to sweep her into his arms. Up came her right hand smashing him at the side of the jaw with her steel-reinforced glove. A solid blow, powered by a hatred that had become vicious. His eyes bulged in astonishment as he fell to one side, barely able to keep his balance. Growling like an animal, he came at her flailing wildly. Up came her left, catching him in the cheek with the ominous sound of cracking bone. He screamed in pain and threw a wild right roundhouse, missing her shoulder. She hit him flush in the mouth, blood gushing, spewing forth. His hands flew to his face. He dropped to his knees. She hit him again, a deliciously satisfying tingling surge of warmth from the contact starting from her fist running up her wrist, up her arm.

He lay on his side unconscious. She jerked his gun from its holster, gripping the muzzle, raising it high, preparing to bring it down full force, smashing his temple. She froze and sighed in disgust. Slowly, she lowered her arm. She retrieved the ropes with which he had tied her, tying him the same way. Then, unbuckling and whipping his belt out of the loops, she rolled him over on his stomach and belted together his wrist and ankle bindings. She took his and Sturges's badges from his pocket, retrieved her own gun and hat and left buttoning her blouse.

Out in the backyard halfway to the barn she stopped short and thought a moment. He was still unconscious. Should she leave him like this? He would be out for at least half an hour, then wake up and flee. If he managed to free himself he would get as far away from Kilbane as his legs could carry him. Better that than stay put and try to alibi his failure to hang onto her. Whatever excuse he gave him, however persuasive, Kilbane would never buy it. He would be incensed. He'd kill him.

On second thought, there was no way he could free

himself, not tied cradle as he was. Come nightfall, after Kilbane and the others had finished with Higgins and Miami, they would come back and find him.

Better he be left as he was; he deserved everything Kilbane would do to him in punishment for his carelessness. Decision made, she mounted Lady, trailing Stanley's and Haverstraw's horses and rode off to Lipscomb.

Sixteen

There was no sign of Stanley Firestone at Dr. Hume's. She found Stanley in his room upstairs over Madame Claudette's. He was sitting in a rocking chair smoking his pipe, reading a month-old copy of the Austin *Statesman*. The color had returned to his cheeks, she was happy to see. The room was small and meagerly furnished, typical bachelor's quarters, no wallpaper, no rug, no curtains framing the single window overlooking a huge and steaming manure pile.

"Holy Hannah, look what the cat dragged in!"

"Well said. Look at you, you look wonderful, a hundred percent."

"Getting there. Damn wounds itch like fury."

"Any pain?"

"Enough, especially if I cough or turn the wrong way." He indicated a small pewter bowl on the little low table at the foot of his bed. In the bowl were two slugs. "My souvenirs, courtesy of Doc Hume."

She examined them. "These came from a rifle."

"Maybe Mr. Acting Sheriff's working Winchester?"

147

"I take it you've been mulling things over."

"I think I owe you a dollar. Either Sturges or Leighton did it, only Sturges would never do it on his own. Leighton's the boss, so it doesn't matter who actually pulled the trigger. You see what I'm saying?" He paused, eyeing her through smoke. "I gather you didn't catch up with either one."

"Want to bet a dollar?"

She told him what had happened, compressing the more important events into less than two minutes. He whistled low in reaction to almost every other sentence. Nodding, nodding.

"Leighton Haverstraw, town hero turned outlaw."

"It's been done before, Stanley. He wants to make something of himself," she added dryly. "Get into the 'business,' get a lot of money, get out, live high on the hog the rest of his days. If it hadn't been Kilbane's gang it would have been the next bunch to come along."

"Ambition's a wonderful thing. How do you figure to break it to Maude?"

"I've been working on that ever since I left the ranch. And getting nowhere. There's something else, Stanley, I think I've made a big mistake. I never should have left him tied up there. I should have. Damn, that's the trouble, I can't come up with anything else I *could* have done."

"You figure Kilbane'll come back, see what happened and kill him? Is that what you had in mind?"

"Stanley!"

"Sorry, just a thought. Not a very good thought, I guess." He puffed on his pipe. "I really don't see how you could bring him back here." She had gotten out the two badges taken from Haverstraw. She lay them in the bowl alongside the slugs. "He'd only deny everything you'd say. Nobody in Lipscomb would take your word against his."

"Nobody?"

"Oh, I would, of course. Mayor Dolfuss wouldn't. Maude sure wouldn't." Again he puffed, sending a hazy, gossamer swirl of smoke ceilingward. "But you played your hand right. You couldn't let him go, couldn't bring him back, what else could you do but leave him?"

"Anybody show up to hold the fort?"

"Your daddy's old sidekick, Captain Devereaux. He came riding in just before sundown the day you left."

"Casey Devereaux!"

"Nice fellow. Tough as old oak, but friendly. Gentleman of the old school, but I bet he's collected a bucket of notches in his day. He's dying to see you. We should ring him in on this right away. You're going to need more than me on your side."

"What a mess. Poor Maude."

"Poor Fancy."

"I know I'm in the middle. How did I get here? All I came to Lipscomb for was to find Kilbane. Look, I'd rather not go over to the office to get Casey. I sneaked into town, sneaked over to Dr. Hume's, sneaked up here, my badge in my pocket, my hat brim over my face. Afraid I'd bump into Maude or the mayor."

He got up slowly, wincing slightly with the effort. "I'll go downstairs to Claudette's."

"Can you make it?" she asked interrupting.

"I got up here, didn't I? I'll get her to send one of her seamstresses for the captain. Did I understand you to say Kilbane's bunch will be pulling out by nightfall?"

"That was the plan, but not now. When they're done in Miami and come back and find me gone, they'll get out fast as they can. If we're going to do anything, we've got to get a move on. I figure we've got less than two hours."

"That's plenty . . ."

"What we've got to try to do is catch them on their way back to the ranch."

Capt. Casey Devereaux showed up shortly. He was a tall, angular man in his late sixties without a pinch of flab on his body. He looked tough as an old saddle. His face was scarred from the Indian wars; he carried lead and old knife wounds like badges of honor. His most distinguishing feature was his voice. To Fancy it had always sounded like soft music floating on the evening breeze. He never raised it. His drawl was not cracker like Mayor Dolfuss's, but deep Texas, plateau-sheep country. He had a way of standing and staring completely rapt while listening. It made one wonder if his heart had stopped and in the next second his friendly gray eyes would snap shut and over he'd topple. He arrived with company, Maude followed by Mayor Dolfuss. When Stanley opened the door to Devereaux's knock and Fancy caught sight of the others, her hand darted out, snatching the badges from the bowl. But she was too late. Maude pushed past the captain, storming into the room.

"Where is he? What are you doing with his badge? He's dead, say it! Tell me! In God's name, don't just stand there!"

"Take it easy, Maude," cautioned Stanley, "he's alive, he's all right."

She gasped, her eyes rising in their sockets. She teetered. For a split-second Fancy thought she would faint. The back of her hand had started for her forehead to effect the classic pose, but it never got there. She steadied herself and glared questioningly at Fancy. "Well?"

"Speak up, woman!" snapped the mayor. "If he's alive, wheah is he? And what have y'all done with the pris'nor y'all stole? 'gainst mah explicit ohdahs. How dare you!"

Fancy ripped her badge from her blouse and threw it at him.

"Take it easy, take it easy, both of you," interposed Stanley. "The boy got himself killed. In the line of duty, you might say. Leighton's all right. He's fine; Sturges, too." He hesitated, biting his lower lip apprehensively. His eyes darted toward Fancy. "They've both joined up with Kilbane."

Again Maude gasped. "I don't believe it! That's a filthy lie!"

Before anyone else could move she hurled herself at Fancy and began pounding her shoulders and face. She tried to protect herself with her forearms. Maude was suddenly wild, screaming, reviling her. Devereaux grabbed her, pulling her off. He held her struggling.

"Let me go! Lying bitch! Filty, rotten liar! I'll kill you, you dare say such a thing about my Lee, my darling husband!"

"Maude, for God's sakes shut up and listen!" pleaded Stanley. "It's true. It's shocking, it's painful. He's turned outlaw. They both have. You want proof, you'll get it."

"I hate you, Stanley Firestone. You're as bad as she is! I'll get you both for this, see if I don't! I'll . . . I'll . . ."

She burst into tears, wrenched free of Devereaux's hold and ran from the room. Fancy started after her. Devereaux caught her by the arm.

"Let her go. Theah's nothin' you or anybody can do foh her. It's just too much foh her to handle out of the blue. She's got to be by herself, get hold of herself, staht thinkin'. Pick up youh badge and put it back on. Nothin's goin' to get resolved with evvybody goin' haywiah."

The mayor offered her a begrudging nod of approval.

"You abs'lutely suah y'all know what you're talkin' about?" he asked, his expression betraying his suspicions.

"I'm not lying, I'm not jumping to conclusions," she said. "I've seen him with them. I know what's going on."

"It was either Leighton or Sturges shot me in the back," said Stanley. "It has to be, Mayor. Nobody in the gang that robbed the bank could know we'd set up a lookout in the alley. Nobody in town knew, only Fancy here, Sturges and Leighton."

"So what's the next move?" Dolfuss asked Devereaux.

"Collect all the guns we can and go aftah them. Unless y'all got a bettah idea." He took hold of Fancy's hands, holding her at arm's length. "Look at y'all, you devil in skirts you! Only not in skirts as us'al. Still pickin' hick'ry nuts off twings at fifty yahds with that Peacemakah o' yours? Ride like a Mexican, track like a Comanche, shoot like a Kaintuckian and fight like the devil's s'posed to be a Texas Rangah, not a pretty little guhl with big brown eyes to break a man's haht, hair like a grackle's wing." He shook his head. "If yo' po' daddy evah knew the way you carry on! What y'all waitin' foh, Frances guhl, give us yo' biggest hug!"

They embraced. "Casey, Casey, Casey, thank the Lord they sent you!"

He laughed. "*Ah* sent me. Let's get ohganized. Y'all can give me all the pahticulahs on the way ovah to the office. The directions."

"What for, I'm going with you."

"Oh no, you don't."

"Oh yes I do! I wouldn't miss this for the world. I don't intend to eat, sleep, even wash my face until I see Haverstraw and Kilbane behind bars. Let's go!"

With the help of Elmer Stockton and Win O'Connor, Casey Devereaux collected eight men for his posse. Three times that number turned down his appeal for volunteers, refusing to believe that the town "hero" had turned outlaw. Win O'Connor was assigned office duty, Elmer and Fancy went along, making a total of ten guns against the gang.

Fancy's heart should have been in the effort, but it was not. All she could think of was Maude, all she could see in her mind's eye was Mrs. Haverstraw running out of Stanley's room in tears. His words to Maude were well-intentioned, but "proving" that Leighton had turned would accomplish nothing in the eyes of his bride. On the contrary, thought Fancy morosely, it would only serve to reenforce Maude's hatred for them both, for her in particular. It was a case of kill the messenger who brings the bad news. A sad and sorry situation with no solution in sight. When it was all wrapped up, she would be fortunate, the very best she could hope for would be that Maude wouldn't come after her with a gun. It promised a long, long time before she accepted the truth and placed the blame where it belonged, squarely on Leighton's shoulders. A long time, maybe never.

"Poor Maude," murmured Fancy.

"Y'all say somethin', Frances?" asked Devereaux, riding beside her at the head of the posse with Elmer Stockton on his other side.

"Nothing important."

"I wish this hill country was mountains," he said. "It's so easy sittin' up top lookin' down on the ones y'all are aftah. Like little bugs comin' scurryin' up, nevah suspectin' y'all are watchin'. I been thinkin', we could just head straight foh Miami. Might get lucky and catch 'em in the act. You did say this Kilbane fellow was plannin to hit the bank *and* the post office. If Sheriff Whittlesey and his bunch are theah now and we hook up with them . . ."

"Sheriff Whittlescy is not overly smart, Casey. Kilbane seems to think he'll sit in Miami until he hears that Higgins was hit. Then ride pell-mell for Higgins, leaving Miami wide open."

"Man'd be bone stupid to do that."

"I'm inclined to agree with Kilbane. Whittlesey's been running all over the area ever since Canadian was hit and by his own admission, he's never even seen them from a distance, let alone catch up with them. I guess he just likes riding."

"He's a damn fool."

"He wants to be the big hero; it seems his enthusiasm is blurring his judgment."

"Double damn fool."

"All the same, we could sure use his guns. It would make us fifteen against nine."

She recalled that Whittlesey had mentioned that Miami was strung along a shelf between a steep hill and Red Deer Creek. She suggested they approach the town from the north side of the hill. Timing would be all. It was better than twenty miles from Lispcomb to Miami. She had left Haverstraw at the house a little over an hour ago. By the time they got to the hilltop and into position the outlaws may very well have finished their two jobs and left. They'd surely be gone if after completing one Kilbane decided the second holdup was not worth the risk.

She, Devereaux and the others could easily arrive a few minutes too late. More time would be killed by the need to ride down into town to confirm that Kilbane had come and gone. Only one thing was absolutely certain in her mind. They would eventually return to the ranch house.

"I think we're going about this all wrong," she said abruptly. "I think we should forget Miami, write it off, turn back and head straight for the ranch."

Devereaux pulled up sharply, the other riders sweeping by him. "Okay, let's do it."

Fancy had stopped. She swung Lady about. "We're going to have a problem. Except for the barn, there's no cover there. It's as flat as a board."

The others had reined up and were milling about them. It was decided that they would hide in the barn. Haverstraw would be untied and brought inside with them to prevent his alerting the outlaws when they showed up. It sounded simple, almost easy to bring off. Which worried Fancy. In her experience simple strategy frequently had a tendency to complicate itself in execution. When the guns started going off anything could happen. Hiding in the barn would force them into a tight group. Fancy pointed this out.

"If Kilbane rides up and suspects anything, just like that he'll have us cornered."

They found Leighton just as she'd left him, his face contorted with pain and so red it was almost purple. Being tied cradle for over an hour could be excruciating, so she had heard; she had never personally experienced it. His face was also swollen where her fists had landed.

"The belt, the belt, the belt! Hurry up, damn you! Bitch!"

Devereaux grinned. "That's the second time somebody's called y'all that today, Frances. Youh reputation's slidin' downhill fast."

Haverstraw was freed. He stood up rubbing his wrists vigorously, glaring pitchforks at her. He extended his hand to Devereaux.

"Sheriff Leighton Haverstraw, Lipscomb. This this woman is wanted for murder; she shot and killed a prisoner by the name of Alfred Gantner. She got the drop on me here, tied me up, stole my badge." He indicated Fancy's badge. "Let's get her back to town; I'll fill you in on all the details on the way."

"Y'all are a sheriff?" queried Devereaux.

"Didn't I just say that?"

"She stole youh badge? Her badge says deputy, not sheriff. Theah's a difference." He turned to Fancy. "Man's face says y'all pack a mean punch."

"Who the hell are you? Boys." His eyes traveled from one familiar face to another, neighbors, friends, among them Elmer Stockton. He failed to find a smile in the lot. The message came home to him, but he refused to acknowledge it. "What's going on? You all know me."

"We all thought we did," said Elmer airily.

"Give it up, Leighton," said Fancy, "you're not fooling anybody. Stanley knows who shot him."

"Not me! Blame Sturges for that."

"Let's cut the palavarin' and get y'all out to the bahn," said Devereaux. "Fancy, y'all and Mr. Stockton'll stay with this piece o' duht, keep him company."

"Who you calling dirt!" snapped Haverstraw.

"Shut youh mouth. Y'all got y'self into this and youh mouth's not goin' to get you out, so save it foh the judge."

Haverstraw's glance drifted to Fancy. A smirk lifted the corners of his mouth. "This hasn't turned out to be as much fun for you as you thought, has it? I wonder who Maude's going to believe, you or me?"

"Casey," she said, "can somebody else go with him with Elmer? I can't stand the sight of him. He's making me sick to my stomach."

"Me, too," said Elmer.

They waited. Devereaux and Fancy stood side by side at the front window. The shadows began lengthening as the sun slipped behind the distant Rockies spining neighboring New Mexico. There was no sign of Kilbane. No one passed, no rider, no vehicle.

"What makes you so suah theah comin' back heah?" asked Devereaux.

"Kilbane paid Haverstraw five hundred dollars to trick me into coming back here with him. He wants me badly."

"What foh?"

"It's a long story. And a fairly boring one to everybody but me. The short of it is he murdered my fiance Richard Ainsley, and shot and nearly killed me. I eventually caught up with him and shot his younger brother, thinking it was him. We've been after each other ever since."

"Tell me all about it."

She did. It took her fully fifteen minutes. He listened in characteristic manner, not a murmur out of him, his body listing to one side completely immobile, his mind concentrating on her words to the exclusion of everything else.

It was getting dark out. The conviction rooted, grew, bubbed and blossomed. They were not coming back. She, Devereaux and the others could wait all night and all the next day, they would never show. As much as Kilbane wanted her he was too intelligent to take unnecessary risks. Anything might have happened to change his mind. Whittlesey may have caught up with them and chased them out of Roberts County to the west. It was possible the sheriff had intercepted them before they even got to Miami, coming from Higgins. There could well have been a shootout. Kilbane could be lying dead in a ditch at that very moment. If he got himself killed his men would scatter; they would be helpless without his leadership. Yes, they would definitely run.

"It's almost nine-thutty, Frances," said Devereaux, consulting a tin-plated pocket watch. It was unusually loud for its size, chopping away the seconds with tireless precision.

"He's not coming," she said flatly.

"Probably got chilly feet. Could be he ran into a buzz saw in Miami."

"Let's get out of here. Let's go looking."

Devereaux's chuckle contradicted his somber expression. "Big country out theah, wide and fah."

"I heard Kilbane say that come nightfall, they'd be heading west."

"Maybe he said it strictly foh youh benefit."

"We can give it a try, can't we?"

"He's carrying the loot from four, maybe five or six different jobs," ventured Elmer Stockton, standing nearby and listening to them. "He sure didn't leave nothing here, exceptin' Leighton. Folks generally do leave their garbage behind when they move on."

His observation warmed her. It was good to know that Stanley, Casey and she weren't the only ones convinced of Haverstraw's complicity. By tomorrow noon everybody in Lipscomb would be. Everybody but Maude.

They mounted up and started out. They brought the prisoner with them, his hands securely tied behind his back, his Winchester fastened horizontally under the cantle of Devereaux's saddle. Sight of it reminded her of her 10-gauge. One of the outlaws had it, probably Kilbane himself. Interesting, if and when they caught up with them and they had it out, he would be shooting at her with her own gun.

Seventeen

They rode in a southwesterly direction through night shrouded, scrub littered rolling hill country that seemed to be abandoned by man and beast alike. In time to their left out of the darkness came the yellow eye of a locomotive sighting its way, lumbering forward, the mournful song if its whistle lifting to the stars. In the distance in the other direction thunder muttered and the wind swelled briefly. The train drew closer, its eye wider, more menacing, swathing the way before it with a pale glow. Presently it lurched and rumbled by, a steel-headed, wheeled and wooden serpent stretched between its solitary eye and a red lantern, like a star fallen and consuming in fire, swinging from its tail. Passing, passing, shrinking, carrying away its low, heavy rolling sound, the silence of the night broken only by the hammering of hooves returning.

None of the riders spoke; the thoughts, the feelings of every one could be seen in their eyes. Like knights of old they were riding to combat, to catch and engage and conquer the outlaw invaders of their domain. They had come to within five miles of Miami, thundering over level ground within a hundred yards of the tracks when Devereaux in the lead drew up so sharply, his horse lifted its forelegs high, pawing the air, very nearly tumbling him from his saddle. Ahead of them a grisly sight presented itself. They quickly dismounted and ran to investigate. In an area approximately twenty yards square lay six corpses and one grievously wounded man, from all appearances within short reach of death and deliverence from his suffering. He lay on his stomach, three crimson splotches discoloring his shirt, his face forced into the front of his hat, the back brim tilted upward, at a forty-five degree angle.

It was Sheriff Whittlesey. Devereaux and Fancy knelt beside him. He had turned his head slightly at the sound of their approach. His left eye showed the telltale gaze of oncoming death. He recognized Fancy and blinked. He tried to speak but could only muster sufficient strength to utter a low, growling sound.

Devereaux leaned close to his ear, speaking softly, slowly.

"Which way did they go?"

"Ok . . . Ok . . ."

"Oklahoma," muttered the captain to Fancy.

"How long ago, Sheriff?" she asked.

A second blink, the tip of his tongue emerging, moistening his lips, sound starting deep in his throat. But it could not rise a second time, softening, trailing into silence. He stiffened, relaxed; his head, which he had managed to raise slightly, touched ground again; he died.

Not one of the seven had taken fewer than three shots. One of their number Fancy identified as Anson Fayles. And a second outlaw whose name she did not know.

"Whittlesey, his four deputies and two of them," she said. "Which leaves eight, counting Kilbane."

"You'll never catch him," chortled Haverstraw, standing at the edge of the group, his reins in one hand. The sickly-sweet stink of death hanging in the air, the bloody evidence of it scattered about seemed not to disturb him in the least. He grinned at her. "You do and you'll wind up just like this. Why don't you give it up before you start?"

"Why don't we tie him across the tracks for the next freight passing by," suggested Elmer Stockton stonily, his eyes drilling him. "Shut his mouth permanent."

Haverstraw's grin vanished.

"Colahful," remarked Devereaux, "diff'unt, pity we can't do it. Wouldn't want to dissappoint the hangman, would we? Let's get out of heah."

They swung about and started back, not to the northeast, electing instead to head into the range of hills centering Hemphill County, running east approximately four miles below the Canadian River. It would eventually bring them to the Oklahoma border at a point where the Washita River broke the barren land. They rode at a steady pace for over an hour, crossing the border, coming to within sight of the scattered lights of tiny Hamburg. They could travel no faster than their quarry over such a distance; with the lead they had, if they kept going they would never catch them. To further undermine optimism there was no reason she could think of for the outlaws to pursue a straight line eastward. At any time, they could cut north or south and having done so, even double back. Only if they stuck to their present route, and, that itself presumed, rode through this desolate and dreary land, stopping for the night in the open, would they have a chance to catch up with them.

She wondered how Kilbane had worked it. Had Whittlesey and his men run into them on their way from Higgins to Miami? Or had they struck Higgins, raced to Miami, struck again and started back the way they had come? The battle had taken place in open country, the area fairly flat, so it seemed probably that one group had caught up with the other, rather than surprising them in an ambush. How it had happened wasn't important at this stage, not to Whittlesey and the rest of the dead, not to them.

She wondered if Kilbane, in heading for Oklahoma, had veered north to stop by the ranch house. Pulling up alongside Devereaux, she mentioned this. He agreed it was logical. If indeed such was the case it would take them a minimum of fifteen miles out of their way.

"If he did go back, I can't imagine he'd turn around and ride back down heah," observed the captain. "Theah wouldn't be any need, would theah?"

She shook her head. Turning in her saddle, she called and beckoned to Elmer Stockton three lengths behind her. When he came up alongside, she explained their thinking.

"If you ride from the house straight to the border, what's the first town you'd hit?"

"Godwin, just over the line from Higgins. Like Higgins it's on the rail line."

Devereaux raised his hand, swung them north and on they thundered. A half hour later they turned east. Presently they spotted a dying campfire about half a mile ahead. They came upon two men bedded down and fast asleep. Wakening and questioned by Devereaux, they turned out to be two ranch hands from Walden, Kansas, on their way to Lipscomb County to look for work. Whereupon luck, that elusive, capricious, annoyingly undependable element that flirts with the destinies of all mortals, but rarely arrives in one's hour of need, did precisely that. Further inquiry disclosed that a group of riders has passed the two Jayhawkers not twenty minutes earlier about two hundred yards to the south. At that distance it was impossible to distinguish one from the other, but the moon was almost full and one of the two men insisted that all of the riders had been wearing Stetsons or sombreros of one style or another save the man in the lead. His hat had been flat on top and rounded at the edges.

"Sounds like a railroad hat," commented Devereaux.

"Moss Kilbane," said Fancy.

They rode on, Fancy and Devereaux pushing their horses hard, widening the gap between themselves and the others a good hundred hards, then a hundred and fifty and more. Two miles from the campfire they spotted a tight group of riders about fifty yards ahead. Trailing the pack, seemingly ignored by the others was Jake Webber. No mistaking his "Cody-length" hair. He appeared barely able to sit upright in his saddle, his body continually slumping, suggesting that he was badly wounded and hanging on with the last of his waning strength.

They were traveling through a wide, treeless plain, Choctaw and Chickasaw country brazenly invaded by Kilbane, likely in the confidence that anyone with ideas of chasing them would hesitate to follow them this far. Still, if Indians were lurking in the vicinity, they would hardly make a distinction between two groups of white-eyed trespassers. One thing was certain. Devereaux plucked the thought from her head and put it into words.

"We'ah gettin' into the haht o' redskin country. Nothin'll bring 'em faster'n a shootout. I can't imagine they'll take ovahly kindly to us spatterin' each othah's blood all ovah theah backyahd."

"Look!" She pointed.

The outlaws had caught sight of them. They fanned apart, spreading wide and going to their guns. Above the crack of rifles and pistols came the distinctly heavier blasting sound of a shotgun. As experienced and knowledgeable as Fancy was with firearms, she couldn't begin to tell the difference between a 10-gauge and 12-gauge. No need to. Either one could blow a hole in her brisket the size of a stove lid. She hit ground too hard, banging elbows and knees, sucking in a breath, muttering and coming up firing. Webber fell from his saddle. Whether he'd been hit in the posse's answering volley or had died from his previous wounds was hard to determine.

In seconds the outlaws were down and pouring lead at their pursuers. The others in the posse coming up behind Fancy and Devereaux were also down, spreading their battle line left and right. There was virtually no cover that she could see, apart from scattered stones, none of which appeared large enough to hide one's entire body behind, and occasional patches of grama and dropseed grasses. Pausing to reload, she threw a glance behind her. Elmer Stockton had been hit in the shooting hand, a slug grazing his knuckles, rousing his ire, setting him cursing. She smiled to herself; if that was the worst wound he was to take he could consider himself lucky.

Her glance drifted toward Haverstraw. She gasped. He had been hit. Unarmed, lying flat with the others, doubtless grinding his body to lower his bones even more, a shot had found his previously wounded shoulder. Blood poured from it and as she watched he shoved his hand under his throat to grasp his shoulder and stanch the flow.

The air meanwhile was fast becoming blue with smoke. A pall formed, hovering above them. With no breeze to stir it it would thicken and spread. The stench of cordite found her nostrils. Suddenly she heard a sharp cry behind her, the yelp of a dog stuck with a sharp stick. She looked back. Haverstraw lay with his cheek against the ground, a gleaming red hole just above his eyebrow.

"Oh, my God."

Maude standing in Stanley Firestone's room came back to her. Again she saw her erupt, becoming wild; again she felt her fists against her shoulders and forearms, again, the vile language, the empty threats and recrimination.

How in heaven's name would she face her now? What could she possibly say to her? Both questions abruptly lost their moment; two shots dug ground directly in front of her, prompting her to shy. She returned fire, taking careful aim, sending lead sneaking under the hat brim of the man closest to her, snapping his head back, freezing him for a split-second in the pose of a preacher appealing to heaven. Then down dropped his head in death.

She threw a look up, then down the line stretched out ten or twelve feet behind herself and Devereaux on either side of Haverstraw's corpse. The two men at the ends were up on their feet crouching, moving off in opposite directions in an obvious effort to come at the enemy from the sides. The one to the left stumbled as he took a shot just under the ribs, his hand going to the spot. His knees gave way and down he went, his gun slipping from his grasp. Steady fire from both sides kept up for fully five minutes. Three of the outlaws were cowering behind their horses down on their sides. A horse was hit, whinnying loudly in protest, throwing its head, its eyes huge with fear and pain, threatening to burst from their sockets. Down fell its head and it lay still. Another outlaw began scrambling toward the cover of the dead animal. He nearly got to it when a shot caught him dead center the top of his forehead, plowing into his brain. Momentarily mesmerized by accuracy of the bullet, Fancy did not immediately see the three outlaws up on their feet, running for their horses in the rear. By the time they drew her attention they had already mounted and were galloping off. Raising her gun, steadying the barrel with her left forearm, she fired twice. The rider trailing threw both arms wide, doubled over and fell from his saddle, his right boot catching in his stirrup, his horse dragging him a few yards further before stopping, lowering its head and nibbling grass.

His two companions vanished into the darkness. Seconds later, the remaining outlaws threw down their arms and surrendered. Devereaux called out to Fancy.

"The rifle!" she snapped, "give it here!"

She had sprung to her feet. He tossed Haverstraw's Winchester to her.

"It's only got five cahtridges."

She acted as if she did not hear. She ran for Lady, leaped into the saddle and raced away in pursuit of Sturges and Kilbane.

Eighteen

Fancy threw the dice. She could not see a shadow of the two fleeing outlaws, but she continued pushing Lady as hard as the little Spanish Barb could leg in the direction they had headed. Both were astride stallions, she had noticed, Kilbane up on a big barreled and beautiful blue-black beast. Over any long run both horses could outrun Lady, blessed as they were with more strength, greater endurance, but for the first ten minutes she had more fleet then any stallion, so Fancy assured herself.

She had covered close to two miles when she slowed, pulling up and listening intently. Up ahead to her left she could hear the faint drumming of hooves. They were cutting north. To eventually double back, recross the border into Texas? Unlikely. What they probably had in mind was to get to Moorhead, Curtis or Quinlan, all three rail stops twelve miles or so distant. Reaching any one of the three would take them through hilly country between Big Salt Point and the tracks; they would also have to cross the north fork of the Canadian River. Their saddlebags had to be bulging with the lion's share of the loot. The ninety thousand railroad payroll alone, taken from the Wells, Fargo office in Canadian, would fatten a couple of oversized bags to bursting. Knowing Kilbane, they would be carrying every last green dollar. He'd never leave Texas and money behind.

She resumed chasing. The thunder audible earlier at the site where Sheriff Whittlesey and his deputies had bellied up had not repeated itself, but overhead cloud cover was thickening, obscuring the moon and stars, blackening the landscape so that presently she could see no more than fifteen yards ahead. She pulled up a second time to listen, then a third. Her heart sank the third time. All she could hear was the soft moaning of the wind.

"Damn!"

As usual, she reflected sourly, Kilbane's luck was visiting him when it was most welcome. Nevertheless, the conclusion that the two of them would continue on until they reached one of the three towns on the rail line still seemed to make sense. Once arrived, they could hole up and wait for the first train through. If this was Kilbane's plan, it immediately called for another decision on her part. Would they head north to Kansas or south back into Texas and eventually through to New Mexico? The latter was the better guess. They could ride wheels all the way to Juarez if they wanted to and by this time tomorrow be out of the country.

Directly ahead pinpoints of light broke the darkness. It was closing on midnight. She was hungry, weary, and rapidly becoming discouraged with the sequence of events that had seen her within shooting distance of Kilbane, pursue him and Sturges and evidently lose them both.

The town beckoning would be Mutual and, excepting any saloons, dance halls or bordellos, would be tucked in and sound asleep at this hour. She would ride on through, thereby sticking to a direct route to Quinlan, on the opposite side of the river ahead.

Mutual brought visions of Lipscomb back to her, the road entering upon a single street equally dividing the town. Light emanated from one establishment only, the saloon. It appeared to be mobbed with patrons, bursting with activity. At least forty horses were almost equally divided both sides of the street at various hitch racks. Not a single horse showed the gleaming flanks that invariably betrayed recent long, hard riding. She passed the livery stable. It was in darkness, the door closed, no one about. She was approaching the saloon to her left when an alley beckoned. Reining left, heeling Lady down it, she emerged at the rear of the line of buildings.

Two horses were hobbled behind the saloon, a big, blue-black stallion and a fiddle-faced grulla mustang. Both glistened brightly with sweat. Both were saddled, but neither carried saddlebags, bulging or otherwise. She returned to the street, hitched Lady, pulled Haverstraw's "working" Winchester given her by Devereaux out of her 10-gauge scabbard and started toward the batwing door. As a rule rarely flouted, she stayed clear of watering holes; it made her feel conspicuous and overly self-conscious entering the company of drinking men by herself. Entering carrying a loaded rifle, she would be more than conspicuous; she would probably stop the piano and every voice in the place.

Which, under the circumstances, was exactly what she hoped would happen. She paused a few feet from the doors. She could hear music and women laughing shrilly, a man bellowing, the babble of other patrons, the omnipresent clinking of glasses and a bottle thumping down upon the mahogany. It was a two-story building; both upstairs street windows were in darkness. A spasm of optimism struck her;

the instant she stepped inside she would spot the two of them at the bar or sitting at a table. Then and there she would get the drop on them and pull them out like snakes out of gopher holes. She rubbed her badge unconsciously with the heel of her hand. Levering a cartridge into firing position, she started forward. She pushed through the doors. The bar was to the left, a solid line of drinkers hunched over it footing the rail. Over the mirror was the customary portrait of the scantily clad and overweight odalisque lounging and eyeing every drinker with a come-hither look. Other imbibers, waiting for elbow and foot support, stood behind those bellying the bar. Every table in the place was occupied. She shifted her head from side to side to check those in the rear. Kilbane and Sturges sat in the far corner, their backs to her. As she had anticipated, as soon as she entered the music stopped abruptly, all eyes were directed at her, all mouths fell silent. The standees at the bar and those loosely assembled behind them turned as one to gape at her. The second drinker from the left was the first to speak. He turned around, showing his star.

"Hold it right there, woman," he ordered. He shoved forth his hand. "Give that thing here, and your sixgun."

"I can't do that, Marshal." She nodded toward the rear. "I want those two men at the corner table. Get them up here and we'll all leave quietly."

Kilbane and Sturges had both turned in their chairs. They were holding cards. Kilbane smiled at sight of her. From all appearances one would have thought they'd been sitting there for hours.

"You can tell me all about it," said the marshal. "I'll listen real good. But first, hand over the hardware. House rule. Nobody carries iron in the Big Bow, male or shemale." He paused and frowned. "What you doin' with that there deputy's badge, anyhow?"

The Odds Against Sundown

She made no move to give him the rifle, despite his outstretched hand.

"The one with the handlebars in the broadcloth suit and the big one sitting next to him. They're wanted for robbery and murder. I've been chasing them all night."

The marshal didn't seem to hear a word she said. He was big and beefy; annoyance narrowed his huge, round eyes. He had taken to breathing sharply as his indignation mounted, short noisy sniffs drawn up through his generously large nostrils. He was getting redder by the minute.

"Gimme them damn guns, woman!"

Drink in hand, he started toward her. She brought up the rifle, freezing him in mid-stride. The crowd gasped. Chairs scraped the floor as people got up and backed away. Fancy sidled to her left away from the doors.

"What in hell do you think you're doin'?"

"Get them up here and I'll leave."

"Put that goddamn thing down afore it goes off accidental!"

She continued to ignore him. Steps sounded behind her, the doors squeaked. She started to turn her head. Too late; a gun pressed hard against her ribs.

"You heerd the marshal, woman, do like he says you to." An arm reached around in front of her and the rifle was snatched from her grasp. The man stepped into view grinning. Everyone else continued to stare transfixed, the bartender rigid in the middle of pouring a drink. The marshal lifted her Peacemaker from its holster.

"That's better. Good boy, Elwood, Johnny on the spot."

Elwood, a gawky-looking, twenty-year older version of Alfred Gantner, restored his gun to its holster. Fancy's eyes deserted the marshal's. Kilbane and Sturges were on their feet talking in low tones to the others in the game and cashing in their chips. Sturges started toward the rear door.

"Stop them!" burst Fancy.

"Take it easy," snapped the marshal.

"I said stop them, damn it!"

"Now, now, let's not have no foul language; they's ladies present as you can plainly see."

His eyes twinkled and he smirked. His comment broke the ice of silence. People relaxed, chuckling and tittering. Conversation resumed. The piano player struck up *Wayfaring Stranger*.

"Marshal, do as I tell you or I promise you there'll be hell to pay. And out of your pocket!"

He sobered. He called to the back. "Elon Potter, Francis Ralph, ask them two gents goin' out there to hold it up a shake."

"Don't ask!" burst Fancy. "Stop them! Right now!"

The marshal's eyes blazed. "Who in hell is givin' the orders here? What is all this? Where you from? What are you doin' with that badge?"

"Robbery and murder, Texas, and my job!"

"Texas? What in hell you doin' over here? You got no jurisdiction in this here territory. You got a warrant for them two?"

"No . . ."

"Then what do you think you're doin' bustin' in here, wavin' a rifle, scarin' folks half to death. I oughta' put you over my knee and tan you proper, Missy!"

The two men he had singled out had followed Kilbane and Sturges out the door. She hurriedly explained the situation. The marshal, Elwood and everyone else within earshot listened.

"Sound like pure bull smoke to me," observed Elwood.

"It's fact. They're killers. They and their gang cleaned out the four counties. That's the whole story, Marshal; you still going to let them get away?"

He was clearly confused. "You got no warrant, no papers nohow, not even a wanted flyer. You come stormin' in here all horns and rattles."

"Give me my guns and I'll leave!"

"You do that. Take your badge and your grief and hive off. This here's a quiet, peace-lovin' communtiy. We don't need no outsiders diggin' up the hatchet and combin' each other's hair."

She got both her weapons back and was out the door, up on Lady and tearing down the alley. Behind the saloon she spied the red-headed Elon and Francis Ralph heading west, giving chase to Kilbane and Sturges. She quickly caught up with them. Elon lifted one oddly crooked arm.

"They're heading for Hackberry up in the hills. They got saddlebags out from behind the woodpile back of the saloon."

"Bulging, right?"

"Fit to split the seams. What's this all about, anyway?"

"Long story. I appreciate your help, but I should warn you, there's liable to be shooting."

"I don't have no gun. Francis Ralph don't either. He wouldn't know which end to shoot if he had."

"You'd better let me take over."

"A woman up against two armed men?"

"It's okay. Thanks again, thank Francis Ralph for me."

She nodded and pulled forward, giving the Barb her head, half turning in her saddle and waving to them. They were slowing to stop and turn back. Elon waved. She didn't need them, she thought, not unarmed. She squinted into the darkness, keeping the North Star on her right ahead of her. She picked up the narrow road. Her thoughts went back to the shootout. She had been surprised and somewhat disappointed that Casey Devereaux had not seen fit to send a couple men chasing after her to help. It may have been that he had too many dead and wounded to see to. If he *had* sent anyone, they had evidently lost her trail long before Mutual. It was just as well, she could handle the two of them. On further thought she preferred it that way.

On she sped over terrain that was becoming rocky. Hills rose around her. The moon ventured from behind a cloud, casting a bluish-white gossamer shroud over the area. Kilbane and Sturges were fifty yards ahead, pushing their mounts, Sturges astride his grulla, game and strong but too small for his bulk. They rounded a hill, vanishing briefly, reappearing presently. The lay of the land reminded her of the terrain where Aaron Fayles and the other outlaw had dry gulched Alfred and her. Hopefully, this wouldn't be a replay of that tragedy. Poor Alfred, he'd never gotten the chance to even start his coveted mustache.

Here we go again, she thought dolefully, two against one. Actually, the odds did not worry her, nor did the possibility that they might emulate Fayles and resort to an ambush. She was too close for that. Her eyes on their backs, both suddenly turned and began firing at her, Kilbane one-handing the 10-gauge. Lead and shot sang by. Lady jerked nervously, her left forefoot came down in a despression in the road; she dipped to the left and lost her footing. Fancy flew from her stirrups.

She landed in tall grass, rolling over. She was shaken, but unhurt. Up on her knees, gun out, she fired. His back to her, Sturges cried out, lifting his gun hand, dropping his weapon. His rein hand, splayed stiffly, started across his back toward his spine. Down he fell. Kilbane pulled up, turning, galloping back, reaching for the grulla's dangling reins. Again Fancy fired. He pulled his hand back, swung about and surged off, leaving Sturges's horse.

She ran to Lady and inspected her foreleg. Miraculously, she was unharmed. She stood pawing the ground, flexing her leg, visibly upset, whinnying softly. Fancy scanned the hills before her. There was no sign, no sound of Kilbane. Sturges lay on his side where he had fallen. His horse stood over him nuzzling him.

She went to him and felt his heart. Then she rolled the body down into the rain ditch. She turned her attention to the saddlebags. So fully packed was the first one she tried it was with difficulty that she was able to loosen the strap. The top flew open. Money.

No money. Not a single green dollar. Both bags were crammed to bursting with rolled-up newspapers. She sat down in the road, overcome by astonishment. Gradually the fog of confusion cleared. Of course, it was Kilbane all over! He and Sturges had ridden out of Texas with their bags filled with the loot, so they would have the others in the gang believe. Only neither of them had any intention of sharing the money with the others. The two shootouts, the first one with Wittlesey and his men, the second against Devereaux's posse had played directly into Kilbane's hands. Let the law eliminate his people and let those that survived be hauled off to jail. When the dust settled he and Sturges, if Sturges was still alive, would return to Texas and retrieve the money, the proceeds from the Farmers and Merchants Bank robbed in Lipscomb, the Wells, Fargo office in Canadian, the bank in Glazier earlier in the day, Higgins . . . Upward of $200,000 dollars, three for me, one for you. She pictured Kilbane splitting it with Sturges. Had they also hit the post office and bank in Miami? Or one or the other? Probably not, there hadn't been time enough.

But all the time, the bulk of the loot had been squirreled away with doubtless only the Higgins money on their persons. Where would Kilbane hide it? Not the dirt floor shack, likelier the ranch house, under the floorboards, somewhere in the barn, anywhere he pleased. To return soon and claim it; ride in, ride out.

She tossed big handfuls of the paper into the air, the breeze snatching it, scattering it. And stopped as intuition sounded a silent alarm, warning. Would he come back for her? His money was safe enough. He had to be laughing himself sick picturing her discovery of the truth. He had played it to the hilt right up to the end, even to attempting to retrieve Sturges's saddlebags, risking being shot at. She had had a clear shot at him and missed cleanly. Why? She could easily have killed him, but Lady's accident, being thrown, landing unhurt but shaken up, momentarily confused, she had neglected to concentrate as she aimed.

He wouldn't be heading for Hackberry now; he would run straight back to the house. He could be there before dawn, stopping on the way only to switch horses, avail himself of a fresh mount. She saw no choice but to follow him.

Once more she inspected Lady's foreleg. No problem, no limp, evidently no tenderness whatsoever. She hat-slapped Sturges's grulla back down the way in the direction of Mutual. Someone would find and lay claim to one feisty little mustang a few hours hence. Tossing the empty saddlebags into the grass, she started out. She had ridden less than a quarter mile when she spied a hay wagon trundling toward her. Up on the seat was a very old man, bent and twisted with his years, clad in bibs so old, washed so many times the blue had faded to an almost chalk white. He wore a straw hat with a torn brim and was puffing on a corn cob pipe. She came up to him. His hay smelled fresh, clean, sweet to the nostrils.

"Good evening," she said, "did you pass a man on a blue-black stallion? He was wearing a railroad hat; he has handlebar mustaches."

He was staring at her badge. He raised his eyes to meet

hers. "Sure did. 'Bout two mile up the road. Flying like the wind. Come straight at Bertha, Eleanor and me. Afeerd he'd slam smack into us. Missed Eleanor by a whisker. Riding hell bent to glory he was."

"Thank you."

"What's all this newspaper all over creation?"

"Somebody must have dropped it."

His puzzled look questioned her intelligence. She touched her hat brim in salute and started off. She wasn't ten strides beyond the wagon when a familiar voice reached her ears.

"Hold it right there. One more step and you're dead!"

She turned slowly. Standing in the wagon bed, showing wisps of hay from his hat to his trouser cuffs, the 10-gauge in his hands pointed straight at her was Kilbane.

Nineteen

At shotgun point Kilbane ordered Fancy to empty her weapons. She obliged him. The hay wagon moved slowly off. Kilbane called after the man, thanking him profusely.

"How much did you give him?" she asked.

"Does it matter? What's important is I've accomplished my purpose. Well now, this certainly has been an exciting night, hasn't it though? I don't know about you, but I'm worn to a frazzle. Oh, before it slips my mind, I have a question. Was it really necessary to kill poor Orrin?"

"I was aiming at you." He chuckled. "Where to now? Not straight back to the ranch house. That's where the loot is, I know, but couldn't we catch a few hours sleep before we start back?"

"What makes you so sure you're going back?"

She shrugged. "Intuition. I can't imagine you'd shoot me here. You'll be needing company."

"You're a funny lady. I respect you; no matter how black the future you never let things upset you. You're just not a worrier."

"I disagree."

"Relax. I won't harm you." He smirked. "Not right away, not until . . ."

"When?"

"Be patient, you'll find out. You'll be the second to know. I'm not going to tie you, Fancy, not while my eyes are open. If and when we do stop to sleep it'll be a different matter. You understand. But please don't do anything rash. I'd hate to have to shoot you in anger."

"I'm sure."

"I mean it. I said I respect you and I do, but you really are getting careless. Didn't it occur to you that I just might be hiding in the back of that wagon?"

"I was too busy thinking about other things. The saddlebags over there, for example, the way you double dealt your help."

"What would you have me do?"

"They risked their skins; they followed orders; they earned their shares."

"They did, only experience and common sense warned me early on that one way or another they'd be out of the game before the final play, either killed or captured. What possible good would money do a dead man or one as good as dead, facing certain hanging? I might just as well tear it up or burn it."

"Did you plan to split with Sturges or was he to be the last to go?"

"Tsk tsk tsk, now you're really trampling on my integrity. Of course I planned to share with him. Unfortunately, he was killed."

"You owe me."

"Don't be grisly. Speaking of destinations, you seem very sure the money's back at the ranch. Why not the other place, the shack Mace Gantner and his people used?"

"Where would you hide it there? Dig a hole in the floor?

A hole outside? It's a little difficult to disguise a freshly dug and filled-in hole."

"You're right. You're very astute. Beauty *and* brains; rare combination." He mounted Lady. "Walk ahead of me."

"Ever the gentleman."

"Oh, come now, Fancy. You ride with men, you shoot and rope and do practically everything else on a par with them, you're a man's equal; why do you insist on being treated like a lady? You can't have it both ways."

"I consider my current status as what you might call temporary."

He laughed. "Very. Me being the reason for it. I understand perfectly. Oh, you'd better let me have your badge." She unpinned it and tossed it to him. "Let's go. I'm sorry, I'm too weary to walk. It's less than a mile to where I hobbled my horse. We're both going to need fresh horses. The first town we come to . . ."

"If you don't mind, I'll stick with my Barb."

"She's been going all night. She'll be ridden out by the time we get there."

"Not if we stop awhile and catch some sleep."

"You look fresh as the proverbial daisy. Still, that's not a bad idea. We might even while away the whole day tomorrow. And go back to the ranch tomorrow night. Play it close to the vest, just in case anybody's nosing about."

She sighed to herself. He would drag it out as long as it amused him. She wondered if he had decided *how* he was going to do away with her. She couldn't imagine that he would shoot her in cold blood. That would be too sudden, unpleasant, satisfying perhaps, but not in the least appealing to his fondness for drama, and no fun. He could hang her; he could drop her down the well at the ranch at the end of a rope and leave her dangling yelling to a deaf world, dying of thirst a foot above water. Various types of executions trooped across the screen of her mind, each one more diabolical and more painful than the one preceding.

One thing she could be sure of. When he got his money he'd be on his way. And before he pulled out he would dispose of her.

They passed a farmhouse in total darkness. A huge haystack stood on the far side of the barn. Kilbane decided that the two of them should catch a few hours sleep. It would also give their horses a chance to rest. He tied Fancy hand and foot and bedded down in the hay ten feet away from her. The wagon out of which he had popped like a jack-in-the-box had just started to move off when a nagging thought crossed her mind. That he ultimately intended to kill her she did not doubt for a moment. But would he first rape her? Outwardly, he disported himself like a gentleman, but his heart was ice. Any man who shot and killed with the ease, frequency and absence of conscience he had displayed for as long as she'd known him would hardly draw the line at rape. It would be more than the means of satisfying his lust, it would degrade and debase his enemy. Violating her, hurting her would satisfy his sadistic streak just as much as killing her. But as of the moment he gave no indication whatsoever that he would touch her.

She mentally crossed her fingers. She wondered too about the saddlebags lying in the grass where she had tossed them. He had seen them but made no move to retrieve them. And yet he would need them when he packed to leave. The two bags on his own horse, emptied of their contents of old newspapers, would not be enough. His sigh broke into her thoughts.

"Fancy, Fancy, Fancy, you can't imagine how much time

I spend thinking of you and all we've been through together. If you've thought about it lately, I'm sure you'll agree we're just about even up to now."

"Even?"

"Don't look so surprised. We are. I shot your fiance, you shot my younger brother."

"You also shot me."

"You shot me. In Eureka. We both survived. You shot at me again tonight."

"You shot first."

She sounded absurd, she thought, the conversation was ridiculous. If he hadn't murdered Richard the entire skein of events would never have ensued. She would have had no reason to launch her crusade of vengeance. No reason to pursue him all over the territories. By now she would have been married, would have had her first two children.

"What are you thinking about?" he asked.

"What you've done to my life."

"How about what you've done to mine?"

"It hasn't interfered with your livelihood, your way of life."

"Oh but it has. Virtually every time I've been apprehended and put away I've had you to thank for it."

"No need to thank me. I was happy to do it."

"You're very courageous. I don't know any men facing the end capable of maintaining such calm, such self-possession. In a way, I'm sorry I've caught you. It's been a fascinating three years for both of us. Life after Fancy Hatch won't be the same."

"Can we talk about it in the morning?"

"Of course. You're tired, you want to sleep. Forgive my babbling. I hope you don't think I'm gloating."

"Good night."

"Good night. Sleep well."

I'll try, she thought. She had one more sundown coming. The odds against her seeing the one following it were getting shorter and shorter. She must remember to pay special attention to sundown tomorrow. Watch it, enjoy it.

Twenty

Kilbane left Fancy tied after both had awakened. He rode into Hackberry to buy food. When he returned he freed her, they ate and started on their way. He told her that his plan was to ride as far as Godwin just before the border and diagonally opposite Higgins. There they would while away what remained of the day until sundown.

It was a beautiful sundown, impressive, singularly memorable. The blood red sun nestled in a pink wall of cloud supported by the horizon. Above it hovered more clouds, stretching horizontally, slender and folding, their bellies the soft, delicate purple of spiderwort petals.

They crossed the border, bypassing Higgins. She estimated that they were less than twenty miles from the house when, rounding a bend, they came upon a sight so colorful and unexpected it startled them both. A traveling circus had stopped; a rear wheel had fallen from one of the wagons. Four men were busy lifting the corner of the wagon, using a bright red pole for a lever while two others moved to replace the loosened wheel. It was done with much exertion and grunting and the pole dropped. D'Urbeville's Great World

Exposition proclaimed the legend on the side of each of the four wagons. They were painted in ten different colors. Painted possibly ten years earlier, considering how faded they looked. An ancient elephant draped with a red and gold blanket with a howdah in which sat a woman only slightly younger than the elephant brought up the rear. The woman's hair was flaming red, her cheeks heavily rouged, her dress sparkling with a thousand sequins.

"Keep going," cautioned Kilbane, two lengths behind Fancy. "Just say hello and goodbye. If there's anything else that needs to be said I'll do the talking."

She was nearing the four men, two of whom were picking up the long pole. One of the other two stepped into the road. He waved both arms. She reined up. Kilbane had to swerve to avoid bumping into her.

"Good sir, madam, are we on the right road to Godwin?" asked the man in the way.

"That's right," said Kilbane.

Fancy sensed that he was about to elaborate when all at once a boy stepped from behind the wagon waving a pistol with a barrel fully ten inches long.

"Stop where you are!" he burst.

He was no more than fifteen, noted Fancy; his gun was shaking so he had to two-hand the weapon.

"Martin, you idiot!" exclaimed the man closest to him. "Give me that thing!" He moved to snatch the gun away, but the boy took a step backward and pointed it at him, forcing him to stop. Both spoke with French accents.

"Stay away, Papa, I do not want to hurt you. Do not make me!"

"*Imbécile!* Put it down this instant!"

The boy lowered the barrel and fired into the ground. All four men shrank back fearfully.

"Quiet, Papa. I am leaving, I am fed up. I want to do

something with my life. I want to . . . want to . . . just stay where you are, do not interfere. You two . . ." He waved the gun at Kilbane and Fancy in turn. "Give me your money. All of it! Or I will shoot you dead!"

"Martin!"

"Son," began Kilbane, forcing mildness into his tone, "let's just take it slow and easy."

Again he fired, the shot whizzing by Kilbane's ear. His father and the others gasped. They stood frozen staring at him. The woman in the howdah began screaming. Others, workers and performers, peered out from behind the corners of the other three wagons. The muffled growling of a lion or tiger was heard.

"Do not talk!" snapped the boy. "Do as I say! First, first, throw down your guns. All of them. If you make one false move I will kill you dead!"

It was not funny, reflected Fancy, despite the trappings, the setting and the characters involved. She dropped her sixgun and Haverstraw's rifle, both empty and harmless. Kilbane also dropped his weapons. Not funny, dangerous. Also ridiculous. She had seventeen dollars. She tossed them to the boy.

"That is all you have? You swear by God?"

"That's it."

Kilbane threw down his billfold, muttering audibly, seething as he did so. The boy retrieved it, opening it with his thumb and forefinger, continuing to hold his gun on Kilbane. Sight of the thick wad of bills widened his innocent looking eyes. "*Mon Dieu*, hundred dollar bills!"

"Listen to me, boy," said Kilbane.

"Shut up, I do not listen to you or anyone. I know what I am doing. Get down, hurry!"

"Wait a minute."

A third shot rang out, the sound crashing against Fancy's eardrums. She winced. Kilbane dismounted.

"Back off! And keep your hands high or I blow you to Kingdom Come!"

The boy had obviously been reading too many dime novels. The way of Alfred and Wayland Gantner beckoned invitingly. Money, fame—rather notoriety—adventure. Even swap for a career with the Great World Exposition.

"Boys will be boys will be boys," she said quietly.

"You shut up, too, woman!"

Leveling his gun, he swung it slowly in a semicircle, threatening his audience. He then agilely mounted Kilbane's horse.

"Martin, you are a crazy fool!" exclaimed his father angrily. "You leave, you do not come back ever, do you understand?"

"Do not worry, Papa, I have no intention to."

"You are breaking your poor mama's heart, *a petit chien!* Listen to her!"

The woman in the howdah continued to carry on, screaming in French, beating her ample bosom, shrieking. The elephant's eyes widened nervously. The boy did not even look at her.

"She has no heart, Papa, she is all mouth!"

His father gasped. "Shame on you! Go! Get out!"

Off he rode, heading north toward the border and No Man's Land beyond.

"I am so sorry, my dear sir," said his father. "I am desolate at your misfortune. I do not know what came over him!"

"Frontier fever," said Kilbane dryly. "Common affliction among boys his age. He took over fourteen hundred dollars, the little . . ."

"*Sacre bleu!* I could see it was much money, but what can I say? I am so embarrassed, humiliated! So ashamed."

"Fourteen hundred, thirty-two, to be exact."

"*Mon Dieu!* What would you have *me* do? Ah, I see, you wish me to make up for your loss. Alas, I do not have such a sum, not near that much. You have my deepest, most heartfelt sympathies to be sure, but money? Alas, alas; oh, perhaps twenty dollars, twenty-five. Wait!"

"What?"

"It would give me the greatest pleasure. I would be delighted and honored to present you with two tickets to our first matinee performance in Godwin. Excellent seats. Front row center!"

"Never mind," he grumbled.

"Four tickets!"

"Forget it!"

"You are too generous, good sir. The soul of charity—"

"Let me tell you something, 'good sir,' if I ever cross paths with that thieving whelp of yours I'll take every dollar out of his worthless hide!"

"With my permission and my blessing, good sir. Farewell, we must be on our way. Godwin awaits D'Urbeville's Great World Exposition. Goodbye, goodbye, Godspeed. May the Blessed Virgin Mary, mother of Our Lord, protect you from thieves and murderers."

Kilbane grunted. Fancy buried her grin in one gloved hand. He cast about retrieving the weapons. The rode off double on the Barb into the gathering gloom of night. The boy's mother continued bawling shrilly.

The holdup was the high point of her day. The day to follow promised the low point of her life. She had had a passing notion to bolt, charge away while Kilbane was busy picking up the weapons, but it would have been suicide. He would have shot her in the back in full view of everyone before she got ten yards.

"I'm curious," she said as they drew within sight of the ranch house squatting in the darkness under the three-quarter moon and a host of stars. "You left Sturges's saddlebags. Won't you be needing them?"

"Come now, do you really think I plan to carry all that money on horseback? I just lost fourteen hundred. You think I'd risk losing upward of a hundred and seventy thousand the same way? Tsk tsk, why must you persist in underestimating my acumen?"

"You're brilliant, I know."

"There's no need for brilliance; thoroughness and intelligence are all that's required in this line."

"Along with plenty of lead, an absence of conscience and a strong stomach."

He laughed. His mood had brightened considerably since the holdup. The nearer they drew to the house the pleasanter and more convivial he became. It was just the opposite with her; not surprisingly. Time was running short. If she was going to make her move it would have to be soon. When he got out the money, when he began packing it his mood would be so expansive he might just let his guard down ever so slightly. If, while he was occupied with the money, he didn't tie her. But of course he would; he'd need both hands free to work. Unlike Leighton Haverstraw, he knew his enemy; he wouldn't take chances in close quarters.

They circled the house, Lady breathing hard under the burden of their combined weight. Kilbane ordered her down in front of the partially opened barn doors. He swung them wide and motioned her inside, bringing Lady in with them. He got a kerosene lantern down from its nail and lit it. The four stalls were empty. Tools lined the walls in neat array.

The loft at the rear had been emptied since last she's seen it, its contents stuffed under it.

"Make yourself useful, Fancy. Start pulling away that hay."

He leaned against the wall as she worked, producing a cheroot from his inside pocket and lighting it, his free hand gripping the shotgun. He seemed to have a particular fondness for it. Practically the only time it was out of his hand was when they were on horseback. He would shoot her with it; the irony of executing her with her own gun would appeal to the twisted black streak in his nature. Yes, definitely, that was what he would do.

She worked mechanically, her heart thumping, sweat starting on her forehead and at the back of her neck. The hay concealed a spindle body road wagon. She had gotten it partially uncovered when he suddenly called to her. She straightened up and turned instinctively stiffening as she did so. The 10-gauge was pointing straight at her. Slowly his trigger finger eased into position. His face bore a strange expression, as if his thoughts were miles away and he was unaware of what he was doing. Then a grim look tautened his jaw, stretching his cheek muscles into prominence. She swallowed.

"Goodbye, Fancy."

He raised the weapon slightly. The twin black circles seemed to push forward toward her. He pulled the trigger. It clicked sharply, harmlessly. Her heart swiveled in her chest. He laughed raucously and lowered the gun.

"You bastard!" she hissed.

"Come now, would you rather I shot you?" Quickly and dexterously, he loaded. "Are you disappointed? What's the matter, can't you take a joke? There's nothing like a little levity to relieve the tension. Now then, get the wagon out of there. Pull it out to the center of the floor and clean the hay out of the bed, good girl."

She resumed working, uncovering a large, almost brand new imitation leather packing trunking standing in the bed.

"There you are, now you can see why I had no need for Sturges's saddlebags. Or my own."

Still holding the shotgun on her, he helped her pull the wagon clear of the pile.

"That'll do. Now hitch up your horse." She blanched. "Don't look so, you won't be needing her."

"She's exhausted."

"She'll be all right, she won't have far to go." He nodded toward the wall to his left. "Get that harness down and get busy."

She did as he ordered, talking to Lady as she backed her between the shafts and harnessed her. The horse was restive. Fancy soothed her as best she could.

"She'll be skittish," she said, "she's never pulled anything in her life. Not since I've had her."

"Well now I have her and she'll be fine. Okay, leave her as is; you and I are going into the house. The back way, the door's unlocked. You bring the trunk." He got a coil of hitch rope down from the wall.

He set the lantern on the sink board next to the pump and indicated the cold cellar trapdoor ring in the floor.

"Open it up, get down and get out the nice money."

The cellar was freezing. No sooner was she down into it then she began shivering with the cold. Most of the money was banded and in large denominations. She handed stack after stack up to him. He packed them neatly in the trunk, humming contentedly, smiling down at her. When she was done he ordered her up out of the hole and into the bedroom where she had earlier overpowered Haverstraw. He set the lantern on the night table.

"Sit down on the bed with your back against the headboard. Hold out your wrists."

"You're going to shoot me tied?"

"Does it make any difference?"

He looped her wrists with one hand, pulling them over her head and tying them to the top crossbar. Then he set the gun down at the foot of the bed and sat down beside it. His cheroot had gone out; he relit it. He drew on it slowly, blowing the smoke at her. It smelled foul.

"Now that you've come into your inheritance you'll be able to afford a decent smoke."

"You don't like it? It's a Jersey, very popular, clear Havana filler. It suits me fine." He sobered. "You think I enjoy this part of it, don't you?"

"I think you're in your absolute glory."

"You're very wrong. That's part of your trouble, Fancy, why you're the one trussed up like a calf and I'm here free, wealthy again and the one who'll survive. If you took the time and trouble to understand me, how I think, how I plan, everything about me, our positions could easily be reversed. The first rule of war is know one's enemy, isn't that so?"

"You really think I don't know you?"

He shrugged. "Evidently not well enough to win. That's the thing about war, somebody has to win, somebody lose. But please understand, and it's the gospel truth, winning doesn't fill me with satisfaction. I have no feeling of triumph, of pride in achievement. As a matter of fact, I sincerely regret that it had to come to this. I shall miss you. You, your spirit, your uncommon beauty. And your intelligence. You're a rare human being, Fancy Hatch, I've never met your equal. Taking your life is cruel; it's a genuine tragedy, but it's either you or me. I don't see as I have an alternative, do you?"

"Can I ask you a question?"

"By all means."

"Must you bore me to death?"

"I'm merely trying to explain."

"Would you be hurt if I told you I'm not in the least interested?"

"To the quick."

"I'm not."

"Tsk tsk tsk, how callous of you."

He got up. He picked up the 10-gauge and levering the top snap, opened it, both barrels dipping. He checked the load and closed the barrels. He held the gun across his front at an angle, the muzzles pointed at the ceiling. Her throat was tightening; breathing was becoming difficult.

"Get it over with, damn you!"

"Fancy, Fancy, Fancy."

"Fancy."

She did not speak. The voice came from behind him. Casey Devereaux filled the doorway. Kilbane went rigid. He started to turn, bringing the 10-gauge down as he did so, freezing halfway into position at sight of the sixgun aimed squarely at his belly.

"Casey!" burst Fancy.

"Keep youh left hand on the barrels, drop youh right, set it down on the floah, kick it ovah; hello again, Frances."

Twenty-one

Kilbane took Fancy's place on the bed, his hands tied together to the crossbar, his feet also tied. He glowered; he seethed; he said nothing.

"Don't take it so hard," she advised him. "You know what they say about war, somebody has to win, somebody lose."

From his expression he did not even hear her.

"I think he's upset," observed Devereaux.

She threw her arms around his neck and kissed him loudly. "How in heaven's name . . ."

"Let's go back to the kitchen, I'll tell y'all all 'bout it." He handed her the 10-gauge. "Try and hang onto this heah foh a change, okay?"

"Tell me!" she burst. Recovering her badge from Kilbane, she pinned it back on.

"Patience. Evah see such a skittery female in all youh bawn days?" Kilbane averted his eyes. "Fiendly cuss, ain't he?"

"Sore loser," said Fancy.

Devereaux had picked up the lantern to bring along. He paused halfway out the door, following her. He turned.

"Y'all ain't 'fraid o' the dahk, are you?"

Kilbane said not a word, continuing to glare malevolently. Devereaux laughed and shut the door behind him. In the kitchen Fancy sat on the closed trunk three-quarters filled with money.

"Y'all didn' think I'd let you run off 'thout me, did y'all? I followed y'all to 'bout two miles befoh Mutual. Then out o' the blue, my hohse pulled up lame. I had to walk her in hobblin' to beat the banjo. I spied youh little Bahb in front o' the saloon so I figured you'd be 'round a spell. I found the stableman, woke him outta a sound sleep. Ornery cuss. By the time I got my hohse taken care of and one to take her place you'd lit out. I asked 'round the saloon and a red-haired fella."

"Elon!"

"Didn't catch his name. Said y'all were chasin' the two of 'em towahd Hackbuhhy. I expect I was 'bout half an houh ahind y'all round 'bout then. Figuhed I'd lost you foh good. Then I spotted all that papah in to road. Crumpled up newspapahs."

"Sturges and Kilbane stuffed their saddlebags with them."

"I know, I know, I figuhed that much. I'm not as stupid as y'all think. I saw the saddlebags. Put two and two togethah. Figuhed youh friend Kilbane was dildockin' his pals and Stuhgis was helpin' out. Long 'bout then I spotted Stuhgis's body. Man was biggah dead than he was alive. I figuhed the money was back heah. I got back 'bout two houhs afore sunup. Found it in the cold cellah. Left it theah. Frances, y'all mind tellin' me what held you two up?"

"We whiled away most of today between Hackberry and Godwin. He was afraid to come back until dark. We spent the last few hours last night in a haystack on a farm outside Hackberry. You rode right past us."

"I must have passed twenty fahms 'tween Mutual and Hackbuhhy."

"You'd never have seen us from the road; we slept on the far side. It turned out the house was as empty as this one. We left about an hour after sunup. There was nobody stirring. And you've been sitting here all day waiting for us?"

"Neah eighteen houhs." He fisted a yawn. "I found the money in twenty minutes. Spent all day lookin' foh somethin' to eat; couldn' even find a crust o' bread. But I didn' dare leave foh feah you two'd show."

She bristled. "Didn't you take a bit of a chance?"

"On what?"

"Me?"

"How's that?"

"What made you so sure he'd even bring me back with him? I could be back there dead and buried in that haystack."

He lowered his eyes sheepishly. "I took a chance."

"Isn't that what I just said?"

"I lost the two o' you. Aftah the papah, the bags and Sturges's body I kept goin, figuhin' I'd 'ventually catch up. When I got heah and found the house empty I knew somethin' was wrong. Frances, what else could I do?"

"I guess. But why on earth did you wait till practically the last second before you interrupted him?" He looked positively meek, avoiding her eyes, studying the toes of his boots. "Casey?"

"Y'all want to know the bald truth? No, you don't."

"Good God, you didn't fall asleep!"

"I was tiad. Ridin' all night, no sleep, nothin' to eat. I'm so hungry I could eat boiled saddle. What y'all gettin' youh back up foh, I did wake up, didn' I?"

"Just in time."

"That ovahstuffed chaih in the front room is comfohtable as a lil' ol' cradle."

"All right, all right."

"Just wanted to sneak a few winks."

"All right."

"Cat nap."

"Yes, yes." She stood up. "Let's get this money and his nibs into town. I won't relax until he's locked up. I won't really relax until I see him dancing. Where's your horse?"

" 'bout a quahtah mile up the road at the next fahm."

She told him about the ranch wagon in the barn. They decided to use it to transport the trunk.

"I'm sorry I fell asleep, Frances, but I did wake up."

"I wish you hadn't told me. It was too close. You took a big chance. We came in through the back door. If he had decided to come in the front." She shivered punctuation. "You're lucky he didn't check the front room when we left the kitchen on the way to the bedroom."

"Why would he?"

"I'm saying you're lucky he didn't! I'm even luckier!"

"Y'all are riled at me."

"Forget it." She shivered again. "I just never want to come that close ever again. Let's get him and get out of here."

She stopped off at Stanley Firestone's while Devereaux took Kilbane to the office to lock him up. Fancy cautioned him to strip Kilbane and search him and his clothing thoroughly before putting him away. The money recovered was to be placed in the safe in the bank, later to be returned to Kilbane's various victims. Fancy ascended the back stairs over Mademoiselle Claudette's and woke Stanley. At sight of him when he opened the door she gulped a gasp. He looked as if he'd just climbed out of a whiskey bottle. He reeked of drink. He peered at her through bleary, crimsoned eyes, got her into focus and tried a smile in greeting. The abrupt change in his expression suggested the effort inspired violent nausea.

"Stanley. I'm sorry I woke you."

"Me, too."

He shut the door in her face. She knocked loudly. He opened it.

"Fancy!"

"I didn't think you'd be asleep this early."

She sat down at the table and started to fill him in on what had happened the previous two days. He had already heard everything up to and including the shootout from Elmer Stockton. She recounted the rest of it. He sat listening, toying with his bullets and yawning. In spite of his condition, he had improved immeasurably. He was much more mobile and looked to be without any pain.

"You got five prisoners in only three cells now," he commented. "The two Gantners from that farce of a holdup they staged, the two from Kilbane's bunch and the big cheese himself. You arrest anymore we'll have to start piling them on top of one another."

"It's just the way the cards fell, Stanley. Too much activity in too brief a span."

"What was it you wanted to see me about?" He studied her and began nodding slowly. "Maude. I saw her at the office early this morning. Elmer and the others decided she had to know about Leighton, had every right to. She saw his body at the mortician's."

"How's she taking it?"

"Not terribly well, I'm afraid. Say, you wouldn't happen to have a cigar on you, would you? No, course not. You wouldn't have a bottle, a hair of the dog? No." He was trying to ease the gravity of the moment. It was futile.

"Did she say anything about me?" He looked away. "That bad, eh? She blames me for everything, doesn't she?"

"I guess."

"You know. Elmer told you what happened."

"Everybody who went on the posse knows what happened. Everybody in town accepts it, even Dolfuss. He was shocked out of his shoes to hear it, but he believes it. How could he not? Maude's the only one who doesn't."

Fancy rose from her chair and wandered to the only window. "Maybe she does only she won't let on."

"That could be."

"I should go see her."

"I wouldn't if I were you, at least not right away. Maybe after the funeral."

"Stanley, how can she blame me? Why must I be held accountable for his actions?"

He shrugged. "You found the key, opened the closet door. Then I suppose you could say the skeleton walked out under its own power. He was a bad apple to start with or he never would have turned. You didn't make him that way. Nobody's saying you did."

"She seems to be."

"She needs a whipping boy. You're elected. She'll get over it."

"I doubt it."

"Fancy, I've known her since she was in pigtails, knee high. She's stubborn, spoiled, petty, a big mouth and childish in many ways. But she's still a fine human being with a heart of gold. And loyal as they come. She's not stupid, she knows what she married. She may not want to admit it to others, but I bet she does to herself. The only reason she's upset with you is . . ."

"She needs a whipping boy."

"She feels she has to strike out, I guess in self-defense. The way she stood here in this room and beat on you, yelling and cussing you out. Striking back, trying to cover up the truth."

"I wish to God I'd never left Kansas."

"It would have turned out the same whether you did or not. If she didn't have you to blame it'd be somebody else. I hate to say it, it may sound hard, but she's the one she should be blaming. She reached into the barrel, pulled out the bad apple and stubbornly refuses to admit it. Closes her eyes and ears and pretends it's all a plot against him, and her. I'll tell you one thing, I wish with all my heart Leighton didn't get himself killed. I wish I'd had a crack at him before he did. I would have busted his jaw!"

"She'd 'bust' yours if you did. What exactly did she say about me?"

"Words. Hot air. It's not what she said, it's the way she's set her mind. Maybe you ought to have a talk with her folks . . ."

"That wouldn't do any good. I hardly know them. She's the one to talk to."

"I suppose. But wait at least a day or so. At least till after the funeral."

"Mmmmm."

He laid a reassuring hand on her shoulder. "Look at the bright side, whether she's willing to admit it or not you're the one got her out from under a miserable situation. You did her one helluva favor. She should be pinning a medal on you. If he hadn't been killed she would have ended up divorcing him. Oh, maybe you did pull the sliver out instead of easing it out painlessly, but at least it's out. And that's as it should be. Some day she'll thank you."

"Some day."

He rubbed his hands briskly and grinned. "You finally collared your friend Kilbane!"

"Casey did. I was as good as dead until he showed in the bedroom doorway. It was much too close, Stanley. I'd already reached a point where my heart was pounding so I honestly thought it would give out before Kilbane pulled the trigger."

"I can imagine. You planning to stick around for the hanging?"

"Definitely."

"Leighton's funeral's tomorrow. I can't tell you what to do, it's your decision."

"Don't worry, I won't show. She'd take one look at me and go wild. I'd be embarrassed to tears. I guess I'll be going. Go back to bed. I'm sorry I woke you."

"It's okay. It's a relief to see you came out of it okay, I was very worried."

"Thanks. Good night."

She walked toward the office. The street was deserted. Light showed above and below the batwing doors of the Bird Cage and the Lipscomb House Hotel lobby was lit, but the rest of the town, with the exception of the sheriff's office, was in darkness. Lady and Devereaux's horse were tied to the hitch rack in front of the office. The road wagon was parked at the side of the building, its shafts empty.

She thought about Maude; couldn't stop thinking about her. Stanley was right, she needed a whipping boy. But it was more than that, deeper. Being a woman herself Fancy perceived things that Stanley nor any man could discern. So her ego assured her. He had said "she knows what she married." She knew all right. The day the two of them had talked about Leighton, when Maude had more or less admitted that his feet were clay, that she exaggerated his strengths and good points and ignored his flaws it was obvious that she had every intention of changing him. Every woman goes into marriage determined to "change" her man in one way or another. Only to find out, usually the hard way, that it can't be done. People are people and other people are rarely able to change them. Instead they learn to live with their flaws and faults and come to treasure their good points.

Yes, Maude definitely had her heart set on "reconditioning" her Prince Charming. Only there wasn't time. She hadn't even been able to start before he ran away and turned outlaw. As a consequence she now saw herself as an abysmal failure and was guilt ridden. It was one thing to marry the man you love and see no need to change anything about him. It was another to marry and willingly accept the challenge of changing him for the better. Maude had rolled up her sleeves and was raring to go.

She entered the office. Elmer Stockton sat at the desk, a handkerchief wrapped around his hand creased in the shootout. He smiled a greeting.

"Welcome home. Glad to see you made it."

"Thanks, so am I. How's your hand?"

"Skinned and sore. Okay. Captain Devereaux's over at the bank with Simms Farlow the president getting the money into the safe. You two did some fine job. Did you want to see your friend?"

They walked back to the cells. The four other prisoners were two to a cell. Kilbane was the sole occupant of the remaining cell. He had gotten his voice back since last they'd seen each other.

"Look who's here."

In the cell next to his Dewey and Hollis Gantner were finishing washing up. Hollis tossed the copper basin half filled with soapy water through the barred window, handing basin, towel and soap through the bars to Elmer. Kilbane got up from his cot and came to the door of his cell, clutching the bars.

"Hello again, Moss."

"Looks like I lose after all," he said smirking.

"I can see you're worried to death about it."

"You don't think you're going to hang me, do you? We've been down this road before. I intend to engage the best lawyer west of Chicago."

"You do that. I'll spring for the best rope in Lipscomb."

Elmer laughed. Kilbane grunted. His smirk vanished. He scowled, his hand went to his stomach and he slowly doubled over. Again he grunted, backing off, sitting down hard on his cot.

"What in hell ails you?" queried Hollis Gantner.

"Stomach," he replied tightly, his voice straining so the word was barely distinguishable.

"He's getting redder than a beet," said Elmer.

"He's faking it."

Again he groaned. "Pendix." Flecks of foam appeared at the corner of his mouth.

"Jesus Christ, look at his mouth. Can't fake foamin'!" burst Elmer. "Man needs a doctor fast!"

Kilbane had buried his face in his knees, continuing to groan pathetically. With great effort, he raised his head. Foam coursed down the side of his jaw. "God in heaven!"

"I'll get Doctor Hume," said Fancy, "Keep an eye on him. Whatever you do, don't open the door."

"Go. Hurry."

Dr. Hume was preparing to go to bed. He came to the door in underwear and trousers, his feet bare. He put his coat on over his undershirt, slipped into his shoes and grabbed his bag.

They hurried down the street toward the office. They were passing the bank when Devereaux appeared at the front door.

"Frances!"

"It's Kilbane, Casey, he's sick in his cell."

"Y'all go on ahead, Doctah. Frances, come inside with me."

Hume had resumed walking, suddenly breaking into a run. She called after him.

"Be careful! He may be faking. Tell Elmer to keep a gun on him when you go inside his cell. Watch him like a hawk!"

"Yes, yes."

She hesitated, then joined Devereaux inside the bank. All the lamps were lit. Sims Farlow was standing in front of his Corliss safe. At his feet was the opened trunk.

"Deputy, the captain here says some of the money is missing."

"I couldn't rec'llect how much y'all said Kilbane was robbed of on the road."

"Can't this wait until morning? Can't you just put the trunk in the safe and we'll figure it all out tomorrow?"

"I'm sorry," rasped Farlow, "I'm leaving for Austin on business first thing in the morning. I won't be coming near the bank."

"Fourteen hundred and thirty-two dollars," she said.

Farlow noted this down on a little pad. "There were four robberies, not counting Miami."

"We don't know whethah they hit Miami or not," said Devereaux. "We'll have to ask Kilbane."

"This is starting to get complicated. We'll have to reduce each allotment by a fraction of the fourteen hundred and thirty-two based on the number of robberies."

"Can't it wait till you get back?" she asked.

"I won't *be* back for more than a week. The Wells, Fargo office in Canadian and the rest of them will be screaming for their money back. And they'll raise hell if they come out shorter than their rightful shares."

He was Mr. Fussbudget, she thought wearily, it had to be done correct to the penny and done now. He didn't seem in the least grateful that he'd gotten his money back or concerned over the fact that so much blood had been spilled. He prattled on. Devereaux had left the front door open when she came in. Farlow stopped short and pointed at it.

"Would you mind closing that door? Any Tom, Dick, and Harry could waltz in here."

Fancy went to the door. She was reaching for it when a shot sounded, coming from the sheriff's office. A second shot followed.

"Oh, my God, I knew it, I knew it!"

Devereaux and she had deserted Farlow, running as fast as they could. They burst in and found Elmer Stockton lying on his side on the floor in front of the open door to Kilbane's cell. In his chest were two bullet holes. Dr. Hume lay on the floor inside the cell unconscious, but he had not been shot. The back door gaped wide. She ran to it and listened. She could hear nothing. She ran down the line behind the buildings, but there was no sign of Kilbane. The music and crowd noise emanating from the Bird Cage made it impossible to hear the galloping of hooves. A full three minutes had elapsed since the second and last shot, ample time for him to get out, steal the first horse he found and flee.

"Damn!"

She walked slowly and dejectedly back to the office. Devereaux had revived the doctor.

"He was sitting all hunched over on his cot when Elmer and I came in. Bellyaching, carrying on. Elmer drew his gun, opened the door and stepped back. I went in. He jumped up, pushed me bodily against Elmer and knocked him flat. He, the prisoner, grabbed his gun and shot him point blank. Most brutal thing I've ever seen!"

"Are you all right?" asked Fancy.

"I will be. He gave me a dandy sock in the jaw."

"I told you I thought he was faking," she said to Devereaux. "What puzzles me is how could he make himself foam at the mouth?"

The Gantner brothers broke into laughter. She whirled on them. Hollis sobered. Dewey grinned broadly.

"You never e'en noticed, didja' woman? You nor him on the floor thar."

"What are you talking about?"

"When we was washing oursells, 'afore you comed in, when thet dead fellar thar was outside, him, Mr. Handlebars, asked to borry the soap. He took him a little bitty bite outn' it. Tol' us what fer."

"Promised to let all four o' us out when he got out," added Hollis. "Somabitch lied in his teeth." He glared at his brother. "Why'dja' go an' give him thet soap anyways, stupid!"

"I didn' neither, you did!"

"Shut up!" roared Devereaux. Uncharacteristically, and so loudly Dr. Hume flinched. He glanced down at Elmer.

"What a terrible thing. All this violence and bloodshed. All so needless. Will it never end?"

"I doubt it," said Devereaux morosely.

Fancy nodded. Tired, hungry, sick at heart, she had a sudden urge to walk outside, plump down into Henry Cleghorn's chair and cry.

Twenty-two

One o'clock in the afternoon. Fancy sat on the edge of her bed in her hotel room fully clothed, turning the situation over in mind, the twists and turns that had brought the whole bloody mess to last night and its apparent conclusion. For Lipscomb, for Casey Devereaux, for Leighton Haverstraw with a vengeance, although not for her. Nor for Maude and their relationship. The breach between them was becoming intolerable to Fancy: if frustrated, vexed, and infuriated her. And she felt helpless to heal it. She continued to believe that it would be for the best for her to pass up the funeral. Why chance making a bad situation even worse?

Once more Kilbane had slipped through her fingers; leaving, as had become his custom, if not his trade mark, dead in his wake. Again she would have to start from the beginning. She had captured or watched him being captured several times, had even seen him go to trail and be convicted. That was the closest he had ever gotten to the gallows. In her mind's eye she had seen it a thousand times—the gallows, the hangman standing by hood in hand, and Kilbane, his wrists shackled behind his back, standing at the foot of the steps looking up at the noose. A thousand times she imagined she heard the trap door fall, the muffled thumping sound and seen him struggle, kick, and die.

She sighed heavily; she would see and hear the whole sequence a thousand times more at the rate she was going. Where in the name of God was the justice in it? What kind of world was it that permitted such an animal to survive and prosper, killing his way to his old age and the quiet, comfortable passing of a decent, honest, hardworking human being?

She got up and studied her face in the mirror. Tiny lines etched the corners of her eyes where her skin had been smooth less than a year earlier. Was her mouth losing its softness? Were the corners coming down ever so slightly, betraying the bitterness she carried within? She had slept nearly eleven hours and was still tired. This she discounted, attributing it to nerves and her mounting frustration at losing him.

Where would he head? He had no money she knew of, but he had friends and acquaintances all over the territories. His skill at faro would see him through his lean period. She glanced at her watch on the chain around her neck. Five after one. At that very moment he was probably seated at a faro table in a saloon in Liberal, just above No Man's Land, over the border and into Kansas, pitting his skills and experience in cheating against three or four opponents. He would have no trouble selling the horse he had stolen for enough for a decent meal, a bed, a shave and stake money for whatever game he turned his nefarious hand to. If he was in Liberal or Hugoton, some place in the southwest corner of Kansas, comfortably distance from Texas, he wouldn't be planning to stay long. What an incredibly vast landscape in which to roam, and how he roamed it! She had caught up with him in New Mexico, in Kansas, California, now Texas. Where next, she wondered? And what made her think he would limit his wanderings to the United States and its territories? There was always Canada, Mexico and all points south.

"I hate you, Kilbane. I hate you so much it makes my stomach turn."

Every time he got away she swore it would never happen again. If somehow, by some small miracle she managed to catch up with him again she would shoot him in cold blood. No words, no waiting, draw and empty her sixgun into him. In full view of a hundred onlookers, if necessary. Only every time she did catch up with him to her dismay *she could not bring herself to do it*. Invariably, she hesitated, invariably ending up backing off and giving the law first crack at him. It was her most glaring and most harmful weakness; she simply did not have his instincts, his love and readiness for killing. It was her Achilles heel and thus far he had made the most of it. She could curse herself for it, she could take a blood oath that she would never let it happen again, given another chance at him, but in her heart she knew it would. And so, because of it, her bitterness was directed as much at herself as at him.

She put on her hat and gloves and buckled on her Peacemaker and went downstairs. She walked through the lobby, through a gauntlet of idlers' stares to the double doors and pushed through them. Leighton Haverstraw's funeral cortege was passing by on the way to the cemetery. She was outside before she realized it. Quickly, she recovered and backed back into the lobby, but not before Maude, dressed in her widow's weeds and sitting between her father and mother in the family buggy, caught sight of her. Fancy did not wait long enough to see her expression change from curiosity to a frown of hatred.

She stood at the closed doors, peering through the artfully

engraved glass until the procession had passed. Curious onlookers across the street followed it with their eyes. Fancy emerged. She stood at the end railing watching the hearse bump along the deeply rutted road. She could see the backs of father, mother and daughter. Maude did not turn around.

She changed her mind a few minutes later. She went down to the livery stable. Luther Coombs was at the funeral, according to his temporary replacement, a boy about thirteen. She saddled Lady and rode out toward the cemetery. Dismounting a hundred yards from the gravesite, she stood and watched the ceremony. Seemingly three quarters of Lipscomb had followed the hearse to the cemetery, most of the people for one reason only, to stand and ogle Maude, to watch her suffer through the Revered Sprague's words and the eulogy delivered by her father. What could Addison Catlett possibly say in praise of the deceased? she wondered. The last few days of his life and the ignominious manner of his death had to be uppermost in the minds of everyone listening. At that distance she could not hear a word, but she knew that Maude's father would find something complimentary to say about his errant son-in-law, even if it meant stretching the truth. The sorriest excuse for a human being had to have some good points worthy of extolling, however badly he lived his life. She could think of only one exception, the recently departed sorriest of all.

She could see Maude standing beside her mother, clutching her hand, drawing the strength she needed to get through the next five minutes without fainting or breaking into tears and sobbing loudly. Her heart went out to her. But she appeared to be bearing up well. Reverend Sprague scattered dust on the coffin, it was lowered, the funeral was over. Maude leaned against her mother for support, crying into her hanky. Fancy mounted up and headed back to town.

On the way she thought about Casey Devereaux. She owed him an apology; she had been hard on him at the ranch house. Whether he was willing to admit it to himself or not, he was an old man. He no longer had the stamina, the trigger quick reactions, the eye, the accuracy, all the things that the years robbed him of. Like many a law man, he was guilty of a dangerous preoccupation, listening to the voice of his vanity when it assured him that he was still as fast and as capable as he had been in his glorious prime, actually a cut better, thanks to his experience. It wasn't so, of course, and it was a rare man who recognized and accepted the slowing down, the changes, the subtle deprivations and made the necessary allowances for them. He had slept too long in his chair, but he *had* saved her life. For that she owed him, and with it apology for her annoyance.

He was waiting for her in the lobby, sitting in an overstuffed chair, his gnarled, deeply tanned hands folded across his flat stomach, eyes closed.

She smiled at the sight. "Casey."

He jolted awake. "Frances. I was just sittin' heah thinkin'."

"Thinking."

" 'bout y'all. Did you go to the fun'ral?"

"I watched from a distance. You didn't go."

"Didn' think I ought to, seein' I'm a strangah in town, bein' with him when he was killed and all. Sorry 'bout youh friend Kilbane."

"I'm getting used to it." She smiled grimly. "He's harder to hang onto than a greased pig."

"I expect youh goin' to be headin' out to chase aftah him."

"I'll be leaving tomorrow after Elmer Stockton's funeral. Casey, I apologize for bawling you out for catnapping."

"Fohget it. It's 'bout time I faced up to the fact that I ain't no spring chicken no moh. Lately it's gettin' so I fall 'sleep ev'ry time I set down. I'm gettin' old, Frances. Still got the haht foh it, but all the rest o' me is windin' down."

"Have you thought about retiring?"

He snorted and waved the suggestion into the rug. "Rangahs don't retiah, they just hang on and hang on until they meet up with a slug with theah name on it. Only honohable way to go."

"It's stupid."

"But chasin' aftah Kilbane's smaht, real brainy."

She had sat down in the chair next to his; the one on his other side had been unoccupied. A heavy man in a wrinkled linen suit with soup spots down his shirt front sat down in it. He was puffing on a stogie and immersed in his newspaper. Devereaux waved away the smoke. A second cloud attacked. He grasped the top of the newspaper and pulled it down.

"Friend, would y'all mind takin' that stinkin' thing somewheres else?"

"Now just a minute, old timer."

"Who y'all callin' 'old,' you blubbah gut!"

"Casey!"

"Get outta' that chaih 'foh I dump you out!"

The man rattled his paper, scowled, fumed, got up and followed his stogie across the lobby. It was suddenly so quiet around them Fancy could hear breathing. Everyone was staring at Devereaux.

"Let's get outta heah; place stinks to high heaven!"

They stood on the verandah.

"It's not blubber gut and his dumb cee-gah I'm mad at. Y'all are ridiculous, you know that? Y'all ought to be bohed foh the hollow hohn!"

"Please, I've heard it all before. From Justin, Aunt Tabitha, everybody."

"Not from me!" He softened his tone. "Frances, that man is one o' the nastiest I've evah bumped into, if not the. I'd hate to face him one on one, and that's what it's goin' to come down to with y'all, you 'gainst him. And he'll have the edge."

"How do you figure that?"

"Simple, the one with no conscience always has the edge, and him, he's ain't even got the shadow of a conscience. I'm 'mazed he didn' take advantage o' you in that haystack outside o' Hackbuhhy the othah night."

"That's not his style."

"It's ev'ry man's, when he gets the uppah hand. What's the mattah with him, is he queeah?"

"I don't think so."

"Don't mattah, he's dang'rous. Catch up with him and he'll kill you. I've seen his soht up and down the tehhitories foh nearly fifty yeahs. They like nothin' so much as killin', the bloodiah the bettah. I'm askin' y'all as a friend, as youh daddy's best and closest friend, drop it befoh y'all staht. Let him go, let him be; with his recohd the law'll catch up with him in no time. He's a walkin' dead man."

"That's the only thing that worries me. Somebody else'll come along and do my job for me."

He sniffed, snorted and threw up his hands. He walked a little circle in front of her, collecting his ire, compressing it into a small ball of rage.

"Then go ahead, go aftah him. Get youh head blown off! I'm glad you po' daddy didn't live to see his only child, the light o' his life tuhn herself inside out chasin' some scum all ovah creation, wastin' the best yeahs o' her life."

"Casey, drop it."

He stopped short; he glared, his eyes narrowing. "I'll see

y'all 'round, Frances. I'm leavin' town right away. Fiahstone'll be takin' ovah the reins. He ain't a hundred puhcent, but he's fit 'nough."

"Casey, please."

He waved her away, shook his head, hurried down the steps and up the street.

She was standing at the mirror freshening up when a knock sounded at the door.

"Casey?"

The voice in response was cold, unemotional. "Maude Haverstraw."

"Maude!" She jerked open the door. "Come in! Come in!"

"No need. What I've got to say won't take long. I saw you at the funeral. I would have thought you'd have the decency to at least stand at his grave side."

"I didn't think it would be proper. I'm sorry."

"I know you didn't shoot him, didn't actually pull the trigger, but you might just as well have. You're to blame he's dead. If you hadn't meddled, if you'd never come to town he'd still be alive."

"Are you sure?"

"As sure as I'm standing here. When are you leaving?"

"Tomorrow, after Elmer Stockton's funeral."

"Why don't you leave now? He won't know you'll be there. Nobody else in town'll care one way or the other. I have one last thing I have to get off my chest. I blame you for Lee, I guess I always will, but I don't hate you for it. The truth is I feel sorry for you."

"I don't need your pity, Maude."

"You're a sick woman; all you care about is killing, vengeance. You don't look like a woman, behave like a woman. You break your back trying to be a man. You don't even know how to cry. You're pathetic." Tears glistened. She sniffled. Up came one gloved hand holding a lump of lace hanky. "I'll never forget you, I'll never forgive you."

She turned and walked off down the hall. Fancy started to call after her, but decided against it. She closed the door and leaned against it. Maude was right about Elmer Stockton. The dead had no idea who would come to pay their respects, and Lipscomb was wholly indifferent to whether she came or did not.

Twenty minutes later she was on her way, heading north for No Man's Land and across it to the Kansas border. The sun had already started down the sky, burning into her shoulders and back, setting her perspiring. She was oblivious to it, to her surroundings, to everything but Maude and their brief and unpleasant parting. And the tears in her eyes as she spoke. Were they for Leighton?

"Does it matter?"

She pulled up and turned about in her saddle. Lipscomb sat huddled on the horizon, looking just as it had when first she'd seen it coming down from Kansas, same road, same point of view. A lone rider was coming dusting up behind her. He sat his saddle with his back ramrod straight, his broad shoulders lifting and sinking in rhythm.

Casey Devereaux. He came barreling up. He was smiling. She detected embarrassment in his eyes, not enough perhaps to tinge his cheeks with color, but it was there in his eyes and in the way he lowered his head slightly and peered at her out from under his lids.

"Could y'all do with a lil' comp'ny up to the bohdah?"

"I'd like that."

"Let's go."

Off they rode.

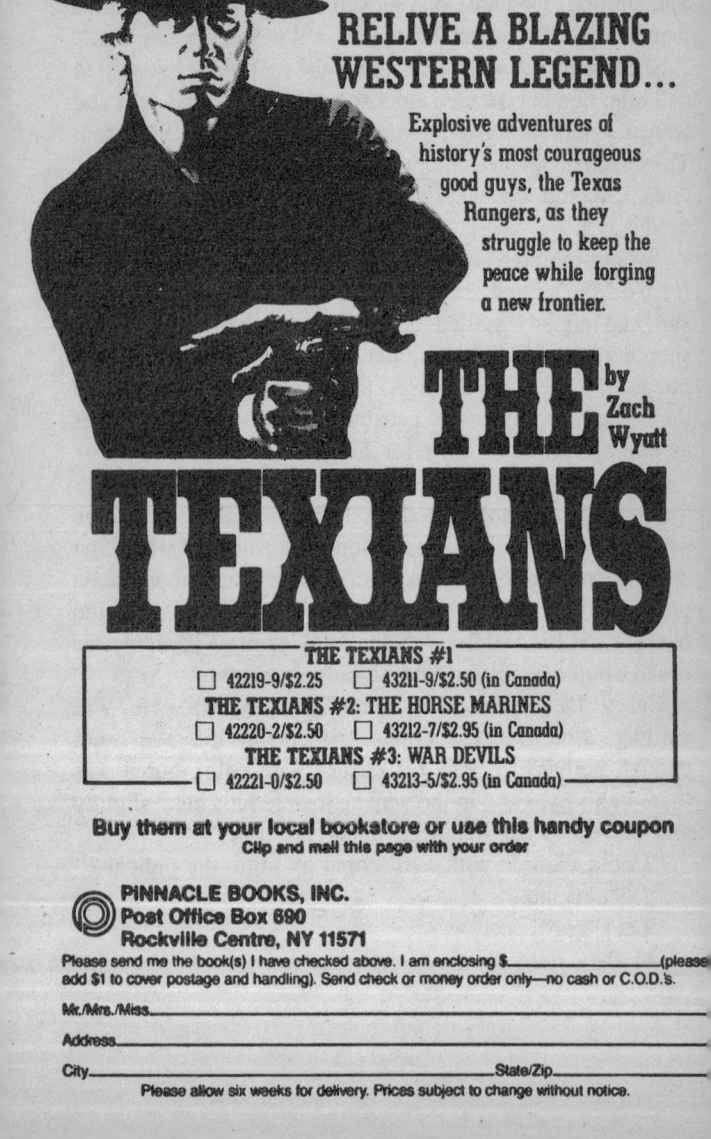